The STORY PIRATES present

DIGGING UP DANGER

The STORY PIRATES present

DIGGING UP DANGER

Written by Jacqueline West

Illustrated by Hatem Aly

Random House New York

Visit us on the Web! rhcbooks.com
Educators and librarians, for a variety of teaching tools, visit us at
RHTeachersLibrarians.com

Library of Congress Cataloging-in-Publication Data
Names: West, Jacqueline, author. | Aly, Hatem, illustrator.
Title: The story pirates present: digging up danger / written by Jacqueline West ; illustrated by Hatem Aly. Other titles: digging up danger
Description: First edition. | New York : Random House, [2019] | Summary: Eliza, a thirteen-year-old ghost hunter, joins her mom on a job in an old flower shop, where she investigates some highly unusual things.
Identifiers: LCCN 2018009731
| ISBN 978-1-63565-091-4 (hardcover) | ISBN 978-1-63565-092-1 (ebook)
Subjects: CYAC: Plants—Fiction. | Florists—Fiction. | Supernatural—Fiction.
| Mothers and daughters—Fiction. | Shapeshifting—Fiction. | Mystery and detective stories.
Classification: LCC PZ7.W51776 Sto 2019 | DDC [Fic]—dc23

Printed in the United States of America
10 9 8 7 6 5 4 3 2
First Edition

A BRIEF MESSAGE FROM
PHOEBE WOLINETZ
Kid Writer

Hi, I'm Phoebe. I'm eight years old, and I live in Manhattan with my mom, dad, dog, and brother. I like to dance hip-hop, draw, play soccer, and write. I like to listen to songs by Bruno Mars, Katy Perry, Taylor Swift, and Kidz Bop. And most mornings I listen to "Ghostbusters" by Ray Parker Jr.

When I'm not dancing, drawing, or playing soccer, I'm writing. I like to write fun facts about animals and the city, but I also like to make up my own stories about a dog and

1

his magical stick or about a faraway land with fairies. I like to write because I can use my imagination to come up with whatever I want. For example, I can write about big men with small feet, and if that doesn't work, I can change my mind and write about small men with big feet. Being a writer means I can let my imagination run wild and make anything come to life.

I like the Story Pirates because they are funny and creative. They take the audience to wherever that story is taking place, and they add in the details. For example, when I saw Story Pirates in person, there was a story about a rock, and I felt like I was there with them at the rock.

Because I enjoy Story Pirates so much, when my mom told me about the story idea contest, I got really excited about entering my idea. When I found out that I was the winner, it was such a frozen moment. I couldn't believe it was happening. I felt like it was a dream.

Winning Story Pirates has encouraged me to be bold about my ideas and to not be worried about what others think. So, for other writers out there, be bold, be confident, and don't worry about sharing what you think. Because your ideas are amazing no matter what!

A BRIEF MESSAGE FROM

ROLO VINCENT

Captain of the Story Pirates

Hello, readers! Rolo Vincent here. Welcome to the second-ever Story Pirates book! We took Phoebe's idea and turned it into a WHOLE MYSTERY NOVEL!

If you came here to read a weird, exciting mystery and nothing else, flip ahead to Chapter 1 and dig in! I promise I won't get mad. I'm a pirate—we're very hard to offend.

Seriously. Flip ahead! Get outta here! It's fine.

For those of you who DIDN'T flip ahead, I have an amazing surprise.

Digging Up Danger isn't just an amazing mystery. It can help YOU create amazing mysteries of your own!

In the back of this book is the MYSTERY CREATION ZONE, a storytelling how-to guide! As you read the main story, Phoebe and I will pop up to point out parts of the MCZ that explain how *Digging Up Danger* was built from Phoebe's idea—and how YOU can build your own mysteries!

Want to see how it works? Turn to page 186 to read "Can You Keep a Secret?" and "How Does the Mystery Creation Zone Work?"

Did you go? Are you back? Pretty cool, right? If you create any stories of your own using the MCZ, we'd love to see them! You can go online anytime (with the help of a parent or guardian) and share them with us at StoryPirates.com!

Ready to start *Digging Up Danger*? Turn the page!

SECRETS LOVE THREE THINGS: darkness, solitude, and quiet.

The docks had all three.

Almost no one used these particular docks anymore. Their lamps were burned out, their boards beginning to rot. The surrounding water was sludgy and black. Pleasure boats had migrated to nicer boatyards years ago. Fishing boats had all but disappeared.

The docks were left alone with their quiet, muddy darkness. And their secrets.

It was well past midnight on one summer night when an old gray boat scraped up against the pilings. Despite the darkness, the boat didn't turn on its lights. The city, twinkling across the bay like a pile of fallen stars, provided the only glow.

The boat was an old fishing craft, just large enough for the small crew that slunk up from belowdecks. Two men settled a plank between the boat and the dock. One of them—a man in a battered sweater, with grizzled hair tucked under a knit cap—carried crates and boxes down the plank and placed them in a waiting pickup truck. When everything was loaded, the man in the battered sweater climbed into the truck's cab and rattled away into the darkness. The rest of the crew slipped back out of sight.

For a moment, everything was still. Black waves knocked softly at the boat's hull.

And then, on the deck, a shadow split from the surrounding darkness. The shadow was hunched and long-limbed,

and as it moved, a pool of other shadows moved with it, rippling like a cloak around its body. It slid out from behind a heap of cargo, glided across the deck, and leaped over the boat's side. Its feet against the dock were nearly soundless.

No one heard those feet anyway. No one saw that shadow watching the truck dwindle away, its head cocked as though sensing something in the air. No one saw that shadow bend, its shape changing, growing lower, longer, faster, until on four silent feet it raced down the dock and along the streets, where it, too, melted into the darkness, one secret following another.

Whoa, spooky! What the heck is going on here? Turn to page 192.

ELIZA STAHL STRETCHED HER tongue.

She was doing it for the fourth time that day. She and her mother were deep in the city now, the traffic around their old green Subaru getting tighter, the buildings growing thicker, and Eliza getting tenser and tenser. She'd already stretched her hands, her neck, and her ankles three times each. Now she was back to the tongue.

To stretch your tongue, you put the tip behind your lower front teeth, the folded-over middle against your upper teeth, and push forward. Then you flip the tip back to the middle of the roof of your mouth and push upward. Forward. Upward. Forward. Upward.

"Eliza, *what* are you doing?" Her mother glanced away from the windshield. "You look like an old man trying to pop out his dentures."

"I'm stretching my tongue," said Eliza. She was mid-stretch at the time, so what she really said was "Ahn stesh-ing mah ton."

Her mother shook her head. "This isn't worth getting tense about," she said, for the thousandth time. "My work at the plant shop should take about a month, and then we'll head straight back home, and you can catch up with your friends, and everything will be exactly like it was." She tucked a springy curl behind her ear. "Two months at most."

"*Two* months?" said Eliza worriedly. It came out as, "Doo muss?"

"Depending on how many plants the Carrolls need me to identify." Her mother couldn't hide the eagerness in her own voice.

"How come they need *you* to come and help them?" asked Eliza, between stretches. "I mean—they own a plant shop. Don't they know what they're selling?"

"Of course. But it's a *rare* plant shop." Her mother's voice grew even brighter. "Sometimes they come across extremely unusual specimens and need to have them iden-tified before they can sell them. They found my name on an article I'd written, and now you and I get to have a little adventure in New York City." She flashed Eliza a smile. "Doesn't that sound like a great place to spend an otherwise-empty summer?"

"It's not the *place*," said Eliza. "I'm sure it'll be . . ."

"Delightful?" suggested her mother.

"*Different*," said Eliza.

Eliza was not a fan of change. She preferred things that stayed the same. Things that were dependable, that didn't grow up and change overnight. Things you could return to knowing you would find everything in the right place. Books were like that. They stayed the same no matter how many times you read them. Eliza glanced around the side of her seat, making sure her box of favorite books was where it should be. There was Edgar Allan Poe, right on top. She could see Nathaniel Hawthorne and *Spectral*

Encounters and *Haunted Homes of New England* waiting beneath.

Eliza loved scary stories. Ghost stories in particular. If there was anyone who was even less fond of change than Eliza, it was ghosts. Ghosts were people who didn't even let death change their habits.

Eliza Stahl was an amateur—and future professional—ghost expert. Her paranormal research notebook was in the box, too, along with her spectral communication tools and her digital travel thermometer for detecting cold spots. Eliza *understood* ghosts. She understood them far better than she understood her botanist parents, who could talk about the shapes of seedpods for hours.

"Spending the summer in the Amazon basin with your father would have been a lot more *different* than coming to Brooklyn with me," said her mother, interrupting Eliza's thoughts. "Besides, a new place full of new people can be fascinating. Don't you think?"

Eliza sighed. She stretched her fingers against the palm of her opposite hand. First finger. Middle finger. Ring finger . . .

The Subaru rolled across a soaring bridge. The brick and stone of Brooklyn rose up before them. In the distance, across a streak of sparkling water, Eliza caught sight of the Statue of Liberty, endlessly lifting her torch. Now *that* lady could really use a stretch.

After several more turns down several long streets, they rolled into a neighborhood of old brick buildings, where the trees were thick enough to meet above the pavement in a fluttering green canopy. They passed Thai cafés surrounded by tubs of tumbling flowers, and coffee shops covered in murals, and markets where racks of fresh fruit glinted beneath striped awnings. And then, at the very end of the very last block, within the shade of a huge ash tree, Eliza's mother pulled over.

Beside them stood the largest building on the block. It was four stories tall, its walls built of mottled brick, its rooftops black and steep. Curlicues of chipping green stonework lined each story. Thrusting from one corner was a turret with a top like a metal witch's hat. A painted wooden sign above the front doors read CARROLLS' GARDENS: EXOTIC PLANTS AND FLORAL FANTASIES. Maybe it was just the building's size, or maybe the ground rose slightly around it, but the place seemed to loom over the rest of the street. The antiques store next door was practically cowering.

Eliza leaned over, pressing her pale face against the car window for a better view, and felt a floating, feathery chill sweep over her. This wasn't due to the shadow of the big ash tree. This was something else. Something bigger, and older, and stranger. Something that was rooted right here and refused to leave.

This place was—unmistakably—haunted.

Eliza's heart lifted.

Maybe summer in New York City wouldn't be so bad after all.

Turn to page 193.

3

THE MAN WHO FLUNG open the door for them was tall and broad, with soft white hair, a full beard, brown skin, and grass-stained khaki shorts. A potbelly stretched the front of his Hawaiian shirt. He looked like a summery Santa Claus.

But instead of *Ho ho ho!* he boomed, "You must be the Stahls! I'm Winston Carroll, co-owner and co-proprietor!" He beckoned to them, beaming. "Glad you made it! Come on inside!"

"Thank you," said Eliza's mother. "Should we bring our bags?"

"Oh, we'll handle that in a minute." Mr. Carroll's voice drowned out a jackhammer just down the block. "Step in and get acquainted first!"

Eliza took one last look over her shoulder at their familiar wagon full of familiar things, now parked on this unfamiliar street full of unfamiliar people, and sent her books a silent promise to be right back. The ash tree rustled with a gust of wind, almost as though it were trying to tell her something. And then, as Eliza turned back toward the doorway of Carrolls' Gardens, something snagged her eye.

Beyond the corner of the building stood a figure. It was pressed against the wall so that half its body was concealed, but the half that Eliza could see was tall and dark. A pool of shadows seemed to surround it, rippling and shifting as it moved—until, in one quick backward motion, it slipped completely out of sight.

Eliza had *almost* seen ghosts at least a hundred times. Unfortunately, those ghosts had always turned out to be laundry flapping on a neighbor's clothesline, or a shadow of a bird, or a strand of her own hair blowing past the corner of her eye. This dark figure might be just another near-ghost experience—but Eliza always kept an open mind. She was craning for another glimpse when her mother grabbed her arm.

"Let's go, Eliza."

"Right. Quit *Stahl*-ing." Mr. Carroll grinned at his own joke. "Come on in!"

He ushered them into the shop. The glass door thumped shut behind them.

By the time the bell above the door had stopped its tinkling, Eliza knew they had entered another world.

First came the smell. It was a deep, damp, leafy smell, the smell of thousands of living things breathing and

blooming. Then came the rush of color: emerald green, jade green, black-green. Green so thick and bright you could practically *hear* it. Green in the racks and shelves and tables full of plants, on the walls and windows climbing with vines, in the lily pads floating on the indoor pond.

"Welcome to Carrolls' Gardens!" Mr. Carroll boomed.

From behind another mound of green, a woman with dark eyes, long pink skirts, and upswept gray hair came fluttering out to meet them.

"Welcome!" sang the woman. "I'm Camila Carroll, co-owner and floral designer!" Her voice, with its faint Puerto Rican accent, was as high and twittery as Mr. Carroll's was deep and loud. Together the two of them sounded like a duet between a flute and a sousaphone. "I'm Camila Carroll, co-owner and floral designer. Win and I are thrilled to have you here, Professor Stahl!"

"*Rachel*, please," said Eliza's mother. "And this is my daughter, Eliza."

"Eliza?" Mr. Carroll boomed a big laugh. "With two botanists for parents, I thought you'd be named something like Rose, or Fern, or Lily!"

"My middle name is Lavandula," said Eliza.

Mr. Carroll's white eyebrows rose. "Well, that's . . . memorable. And you're how old? Thirteen?"

Eliza nodded.

"Did you hear that, Tommy?" Mr. Carroll called. Eliza couldn't have imagined Mr. Carroll's voice getting any louder, but now it made her back teeth vibrate. "Just a little bit younger than you! Come here and say hello!"

A teenaged boy shuffled into the room. He had olive skin, thick dark hair hanging over one eye, and arms full of bagged peat moss. Maybe because of the moss—or the hair—he walked straight into a rack of orchids.

Mrs. Carroll caught the rack before it could tip. "This is our nephew, Tommy. He's living with us and working here for the summer."

"Thomas," mumbled the boy. "Mice to neat you."

Eliza bit back a nervous giggle.

"Tommy," said Mrs. Carroll sweetly, "why don't you see to any customers while Win and I get the Stahls settled upstairs?"

"We'll have you planted in no time!" boomed Mr. Carroll.

Two minutes later, wearing her backpack and carrying her box of books, Eliza found herself following Mrs. Carroll's fluttering skirts across the shop's front room. A whirl of new, sweeter smells greeted her as they entered the cut flower department. Tubs of bright flowers cluttered the floor. Buckets of roses and mums formed fireworks of color behind foggy glass refrigerator doors. A cluster of lilies spilled from a vase on the countertop.

"This is where you'll usually find me, with my face buried in a bouquet," said Mrs. Carroll happily, leading the way up the staircase that angled through the floral department. "If you get close enough to flowers, you can practically hear them singing to you."

"What do they sing?" Eliza asked curiously.

"Oh, not songs," said Mrs. Carroll. "Each one just sings its own little note. But when you put a bunch of them together, you can hear chords. *Symphonies*."

Eliza glanced back at her mother, who was trying very hard to straighten a smirk.

"We live here on the second floor, Camila and Tommy and I," boomed Mr. Carroll, as they crossed a landing onto another flight of stairs. Through an open doorway, Eliza caught a flash of colorful rugs and squishy furniture.

"We have the whole building," Mrs. Carroll explained over one shoulder. "It's been in Win's family for ages."

"Yes, we put down roots here a long time ago!" Mr. Carroll laughed.

The next flight of stairs was narrower and creakier. The hallway it led to was dim. The surrounding air was cool, which might have been due to the thick brick walls, or—possibly—to spectral presences. Eliza held her box tight, squinting eagerly through the shadows.

"Most of this floor is shop storage," said Mrs. Carroll, leading the way past a row of bolted wooden doors. "But the best part of it is all yours!"

She threw open the door at the very end of the hall.

Eliza and her mother stepped over the threshold.

The room they entered was large and high-ceilinged, with dark green paper coating the walls. Narrow windows glowed with dusty sunlight. A tiny stove and an old enamel sink sat in one corner. A table with two chairs stood in the center of the room, a spindly chandelier dangling above it like a big glass spider. At the far end of the room, two wrought-iron beds—the kind that creaked every time a person twitched in her sleep—were covered in patchwork quilts. Thrusting out from the remaining corner, its interior a shadowy half-circle lined with cushioned seats, was the pointy turret.

"We used to rent out this room, but we gave up that bother a few years ago," Mrs. Carroll was saying. "We know it's a bit outdated. . . ."

But Eliza wasn't listening. She was staring at the turret, at the chandelier, at all the shadowy nooks where ghosts could hide. Her family's house in Massachusetts had only been built in 1950. It was full of clean angles and smooth walls and floors that didn't creak, and it stood on a street of other creak-less houses. When her parents had explained that, as far as they knew, no one had ever died a horrible death inside of it, Eliza had been seriously disappointed. But this place was so rambling and old and odd, it had to have at least one ghost hanging around. Maybe more than one. Maybe a whole ghost family. Eliza's skin zinged with excitement.

"This is lovely," said Eliza's mother, but in a way that told Eliza she'd be checking for black mold later.

"Would you like some time to unpack and freshen up?" asked Mrs. Carroll.

"Honestly, I'm dying to get a look at your plants." Eliza's mother swung her laptop bag over her shoulder. "Do you mind if I just jump in?"

"Do we *mind*?" Mr. Carroll boomed. "We *hoped* you'd say that! We've got a whole room full of mystery plants just waiting for you!"

Mr. and Mrs. Carroll bustled back into the hall, followed by Eliza's mother.

Eliza was taking a last look around when, from some- where nearby, there came a soft creak.

Eliza froze.

The sound hadn't come from the hallway. In fact, if she had to guess, Eliza would have said it came from directly above. She looked up at the cracked plaster ceiling. Was it just the creaking of a weathered old building? If not ... what was up there?

"Eliza!" Her mother's voice sliced through the silence. "Come with us, please!"

Eliza sighed. "Coming!" she called back, and hurried through the door after the others.

Now we're really setting the scene for a mystery. Turn to page 194.

"**O**UR PLANTS COME IN from all over the world," said Mr. Carroll, as they thumped back through the floral department into the shop's main room. A few customers browsed the shelves. Tommy was nowhere in sight. "We've got things no one else carries," he went on. "Things no one else has ever seen—Camila and I included, and we've seen a few plants! A few years ago, we found a botanist who was willing to help us determine care preferences, observe interesting properties—poisonous, edible, self-pollinating, what have you. When he moved away, we were really up a tree."

"Thank goodness you've come to save us!" said Mrs. Carroll. "You too, Eliza." She gave her a twinkly smile. "Summer is our busiest season. We're so grateful for an extra pair of hands around the shop!"

Mr. Carroll opened a door tucked away in one shady

corner. "Here it is." He dropped his voice dramatically. "The treasure chamber."

Everyone stepped through the doorway.

Eliza glanced around. The room was smallish, with a row of latticed windows letting in the sunlight. Except for one tall laboratory table in the middle, every bit of the room was crammed with plants. Very *weird* plants. Plants with purple-veined leaves and huge fuchsia flowers. Plants with three-inch black thorns. Plants that sent out tendrils as fine as spiderweb to coil around anything that wandered near.

Eliza's mother gave the kind of sigh she usually gave when she took her first sip of coffee in the morning.

She made a beeline toward the nearest specimen. Eliza watched her do the things she always did when she examined an interesting plant: crouching down, squinting, darting from side to side like a giant frizzy-haired hummingbird.

"Please make yourself at home," said Mrs. Carroll. "Although we can't advise you to touch anything. We don't know what stings and what doesn't!"

Eliza's mother paused in front of something that looked like a miniature birch tree, except that its leaves were a vivid gold, and clusters of glittering red berries dangled from its twigs. She darted in for a closer look. "This is stunning," she said. "Do you know where it came from?"

"Somewhere in North America, I believe!" Mr. Carroll

gave a big shrug and another chuckle. "Like I said, our dealers cover the whole globe. That's the one I'm most curious about myself. Never seen anything like it."

"Stunning," said Eliza's mother again.

Eliza edged around the room. She backed away from a cluster of plants that looked like they might bite and skirted something with a speckled seed pod as long as her arm. She was bending down to sniff a wrinkly blue flower when, from somewhere nearby, there came a deep, ghostly moan.

Eliza froze.

A second strange sound within ten minutes? This place was definitely ripe for paranormal research!

She glanced over her shoulder. No one else had turned toward the sound. Her mother and the Carrolls were still staring at the little red-gold tree, not acting at all like people who'd just heard a ghost.

But Eliza knew that people often don't notice what they don't expect to notice.

She peered into the leafy shadows. When she took a small step sideways, the moan came again, a bit louder. It had a breathiness to it, a sort of tired ache. And it seemed to be coming from the floor.

Maybe there was a vent in the floorboards. The vent could lead down to the basement—which, after an attic, would be a ghost's favorite lurking place.

Eliza crouched down to look.

There was no vent. There was something else.

From the darkness beneath a rack of plants, a black blob with gleaming yellow eyes stared straight back at her.

Eliza yelped.

She jumped backward. Her heel hit a giant potted fern, and she toppled through its rustling branches, plunking onto her behind on its other side.

Now everybody turned to look.

"Oh, I see you've met Moggie!" sang Mrs. Carroll. She swept across the room, jewelry jingling. "She's an opinionated old thing, our Moggie-doggie." She bent down to rub the ears of what Eliza now saw was an ancient black dog. "She's the one who's really in charge around here."

Eliza blinked at the dog. It was about the size of a retriever, with a long snout, droopy gold eyes, and black hair frosted with puffs of gray. Eliza didn't know much about dogs, but as far as she could see, this one didn't look like it was in charge of anything—including its own tail, which was banging floppily against one table leg. Mrs. Carroll went on rubbing, and the dog let out another low groan.

A mixture of relief and disappointment washed through Eliza's chest, dragging her heartbeat back to normal. Oh well. One more *almost* ghost sighting was better than no sighting at all.

That ghostly moan got my heart racing! Turn to page 201.

"Eliza, I'll be busy here for a while." Her mother was setting out her notebooks with one hand while bundling her hair into a knot with the other. "You could get to work, too. I'm sure the Carrolls can tell you where to start."

Before Eliza could answer, Mrs. Carroll sang, "Oh, Tommy can show you around. Where did that boy go? Tommy? *Tommy!*"

Tommy slumped into the doorway, gazing at them through a curtain of hair.

"Tommy, why don't you give Eliza a tour of the shop?" said Mrs. Carroll. "Then she can help you with the repotting or deadheading or whatever needs doing."

Behind their hair curtain, Tommy's eyes widened with dread. "Uh . . ."

"He doesn't have to," Eliza blurted. "I mean, I can just—"

"That would be perfect," said Eliza's mother loudly. She looked up from her work, straight into Eliza's eyes. "Eliza is happy to help with whatever needs doing. Right, Eliza?"

"Right," said Eliza. "I just—"

"Lovely!" exclaimed Mrs. Carroll. "Go ahead, you two!"

Tommy turned and shuffled off. Eliza slunk after him, stretching her fingers against her opposite palm one by one.

There was nothing so bad about Tommy. But he was clearly uncomfortable with her, and that made Eliza even more uncomfortable with *him*. Maybe Tommy liked things that stayed the same, too—not strange people who blew into your life and bumped everything out of its usual place. Or maybe he just didn't like *her*. Eliza stretched her fingers harder.

Tommy led the way through the main room. Even with customers browsing here and there, the room was hushed, like a garden with no birds or breeze.

Tommy stopped beside the counter, pointed at a phone, and mumbled something that sounded like *foam*. He tapped a board below the register counter, where keys hung on little brass hooks labeled FRONT DOOR, BASEMENT, ATTIC, THIRD FLOOR ROOM, and RESTROOM. "Spare keys," he mumbled.

Then he wheeled around, almost smacked straight into Eliza, shook his hair back over his face, and shuffled off in another direction.

Eliza followed him, keeping a careful distance. Tommy reminded her of a teenage version of Cousin Itt from *The Addams Family*. She'd always wondered how Itt had gotten around without walking into things.

Barely skirting a rack of cacti, Tommy shuffled through an archway into another high-ceilinged room. At least, Eliza assumed it was a room. If not for the creaky floor under their feet, it could have been a patch of forest.

Potted trees with speckled leaves and glassy black fruits reached all the way to the canopied ceiling. Giant shrubs filled the corners. Vines tangled on the walls. The air was humid and clogged with scents—scents that reminded Eliza of lemons and smoke and rotting meat, but that must have been coming from the blossoms nearby. Eliza leaned down and sniffed a red flower. Yep. Rotting sausage.

"Popular plants are out front," said Tommy, in a voice so soft Eliza almost missed it. "These are the rarer ones. Things almost nobody buys."

Eliza gazed down at something that looked like a haystack made of mold. "Who *does* buy them?"

"Plant collectors." Tommy shrugged. "Weird rich people."

"Is there anything *really* strange?" Eliza asked. "Like, anything you have to water with your own blood?"

"This isn't *Little Shop of Horrors*."

Eliza glanced up. Behind the oily brown curtain of his hair, Tommy seemed to be *almost* smiling. She almost-smiled back.

"I'm not really into plants," she admitted. "But I like scary stories."

Tommy looked down again, as though her eyes had shoved his away. "I like *The Twilight Zone*," he mumbled to his shoes. "Well. Um. We'd better keep going."

He lurched through the room toward another open doorway.

They made their way along a narrow hall. They passed a door marked STAFF ONLY, and another door marked RESTROOM— SEE STAFF FOR KEY, and a heavier, wider wooden door marked NO ADMITTANCE.

"What's through there?" Eliza asked.

"Um . . ." Tommy glanced back. "The basement."

"Is it a creepy basement?" Eliza asked eagerly. "Like—do you ever see things moving in the corners, but when you turn around, nothing's there?"

Tommy threw a wary look in her direction. "No."

"Never?"

"No."

Eliza's heart sank.

"It's mostly just soil and fertilizer and chemicals." Tommy pointed to the end of the hall. "There's the door to the backyard."

"There's a backyard?" Eliza had thought houses in the city didn't have yards at all.

"A little one. Behind the greenhouse."

"There's a greenhouse?"

Tommy didn't answer. He just pushed open a pair of glass doors.

A wall of damp air smacked Eliza in the face. The smell of the plants had been strong in the rest of the shop, but here, it was so green and forceful she could practically feel it shooting into her lungs. Behind it came the rich, murky smell of the soil. Inhaling the air of the greenhouse was less like breathing and more like sucking a garden up into your nose. It made her woozy.

Tommy threaded through the glass house, dodging plant-packed tables and hanging baskets. "We can start deadheading here."

Eliza glanced around the greenhouse. She wasn't sure

what she was looking for, but it might have been a miniature guillotine. "How do you do it?"

Tommy reached for the nearest plant, gently tugging off a withered blossom and tossing it into a compost bin. "You take off any dead flowers."

"That's it?" said Eliza. "*Deadheading* sounds so . . . violent."

"Don't you know everything about plants already?" Tommy asked Eliza's shoes. "With your mom, I mean?"

"She and my dad tried to get me interested, but it never really worked." Eliza watched Tommy pluck a crumpled flower. "Why do you know this stuff? Because of your family?"

Tommy shrugged. "Some, I guess. I just—I like botany. Biology. Ecology. How things affect each other." He broke off with a little flinch, like all the words he'd just spoken had startled him. He shook his hair back over his eyes. "So. Um. You can do that side. I'll do this one."

They got to work, back to back. Eliza was sick of deadheading in about two minutes, but she figured that she shouldn't complain about her very first chore on her very first day, so she kept quiet. Tommy kept quiet, too. The longer the quiet went on, the more *real* it seemed. Soon Eliza could practically feel it looming behind her, just out of sight, like a ghostly presence.

Eliza would have picked a ghostly presence over human quiet any day.

Ghosts were nothing to be feared. They were just souls who wanted to stay where they had always belonged. It was

31

people who could be trouble. It was people who could stick out a foot and trip you, or decide they weren't your best friends anymore, or give you such relentless silent treatment that your whole body got as tense as a strained rubber band.

Eliza stretched her neck. She stretched her shoulders. She reached for a withered blossom and accidentally ripped off a live one instead.

She glanced around to see if Tommy had noticed.

But Tommy wasn't there.

He wasn't anywhere in the greenhouse. She and the plants were alone. The silence, which she thought she'd been sharing with someone, seemed suddenly crushing, all of its weight falling onto her alone. Its pressure filled the dewy air.

Eliza turned in a slow circle. How long had she been alone? A few minutes? Longer? Had Tommy rushed away as soon as he got the chance? She held her breath, listening, but in the insulated greenhouse, she couldn't hear a thing. No footsteps. No voices from inside the shop. Not even the noise of the street beyond this weird green world.

From the corner of her eye, she saw something move—a streak of shadow outside the misty glass walls. The shadow seemed too low and too long to be Tommy's. Probably just Moggie lumbering through the backyard, Eliza told herself. She waited, watching. But whatever it was had vanished. And Tommy didn't return.

THE CARROLLS INSISTED THAT the Stahls join them for dinner that night. At closing time, they all trooped up to the second-floor apartment, where Mr. Carroll's pot of jollof rice sent out ribbons of spicy scent.

Eliza would have preferred a meal she'd had a thousand times before, like her father's Monday Macaroni or Tuesday Tacos, or her mom's Wednesday Western Omelette. But the rice turned out to be pretty tasty.

They all clustered around the Carrolls' table and ate and made small talk. The adults made small talk, anyway. Tommy and Eliza mostly just ate. Tommy had never returned to the greenhouse. Eliza had eventually found him tending orchids in the front room, and he'd looked almost startled to see her, like he'd already forgotten she was there. Moggie lay between their feet under the dinner table, giving occasional wheezes. Mr. Carroll slipped her a bit of chicken whenever Mrs. Carroll wasn't looking. Mrs.

Carroll did the same thing whenever Mr. Carroll wasn't looking. And when Tommy wasn't looking, Moggie craned up and slurped a chunk of chicken off the edge of his plate.

Finally, Mr. Carroll brought a heaping plate of brownies out of the kitchen, plunked back down in his chair, and boomed, "Well, Professor, we're dying to know what you think! Anything you can tell us yet?"

Eliza's mother clasped her hands on the tabletop. Eliza knew exactly how this went: The longer her mother talked, the livelier and more expressive her hands would get. She'd seen them smack hanging light fixtures and accidentally slap strangers. Eliza leaned back in her chair.

"Well," her mother began, her fingers starting to twitch, "you have several specimens I've never seen before, even in photographs. That variegated fern, for example. I'd love to know if it's a mutation of some kind, or if it's a trait of its entire genus. There's another that may be a dwarf ginkgo, but of a variety I've never seen. And of course there's the plant with the rufous fruits. . . ."

Her mother continued, using words like *abaxial* and *unilocular* and *exocarp*, punctuated by bigger and bigger gestures. By the time she got to *drupelet*, she'd bumped Eliza's arm twice and nearly toppled a water glass.

Eliza glanced around. Mr. and Mrs. Carroll were nodding and beaming. Tommy was listening intently, his eyes gleaming behind his oily hair. Moggie was licking his plate.

"And I'm just getting started," said Eliza's mother. "I haven't used the microscope yet, or sectioned any fruits, or contacted any colleagues for their input. But I'll—"

"Oh, we'd prefer if you *didn't* talk with anyone about our plants," said Mrs. Carroll, in such a sweetly apologetic tone that it didn't even seem like an interruption.

Her mother's hands dropped to the tabletop. "You don't want me to confer with other botanists?"

"If you don't mind," said Mr. Carroll. "Brownie?" He wafted the plate under her nose.

Eliza's mother took a bite. "I don't mind, if you . . ." Her eyes slid partly shut. "Are there dark chocolate chips in this?"

"Dark *and* milk chocolate," said Mrs. Carroll.

Her mother took another bite. "I can certainly . . . *Mmm* . . . I can continue my work alone. But having other experts weigh in may give you better conclusions."

"We'll trust *your* conclusions," said Mrs. Carroll. "The truth is, we don't want too much information about our very rarest plants flying around. We've got our own loyal buyers, and our own special dealers, and we'd like to keep a few little trade secrets. You understand."

"It's your choice, of course," said Eliza's mother. "I just hope I'll be enough help on my own."

Mrs. Carroll laughed. "Oh, Professor Stahl, we're not worried about that one bit."

"Enough shop talk. What about *you*?" said Mr. Carroll abruptly, turning to Eliza with a wide, warm smile. "What are your hobbies? Botany? Zoology? Paleontology?"

"Um . . . ," said Eliza. "Not any of those."

"Of course not, Win." Mrs. Carroll gave her husband a swat on the arm. "She's a thirteen-year-old girl! She probably plays sports, or dances, or sings." She turned her own smile on Eliza. "Am I a better guesser than the big goofball beside me?"

"Actually," Eliza began, "I'm mostly interested in psychical research." The Carrolls' eyebrows rose simultaneously.

"Psychology?" said Mr. Carroll.

"No, like—paranormal investigation," Eliza explained. "Ghost hunting."

"Pseudoscience," said her mother to the Carrolls, in the way other people would say *diarrhea*.

"Just because something isn't proven *yet* doesn't mean it

won't be," Eliza argued. "Isn't that what scientists do? Collect data and test theories?"

Mr. Carroll tipped his head thoughtfully. "I suppose you're right."

"And lots of things people used to think were crazy or magical have turned out to be completely real," Eliza pushed on. "Like that people can come back from the dead, by waking up from comas. Or that humans can walk on the moon. Or that plants can communicate."

Eliza's mother sighed. But the Carrolls were both nodding. And Tommy was staring steadily at her. Until now, he hadn't ever looked at her long enough for her to notice the hazel color of his eyes.

"I just think it's *interesting*," Eliza finished. "I think it's something waiting to be discovered."

"Hmm." Mr. Carroll leaned back in his chair. "You know, you may have come to just the right place."

"Win," said Mrs. Carroll warningly.

"This is one of the oldest parts of the city," Mr. Carroll went on. "People have been settling here for centuries. Millennia. Just think of the history. The number of people who've lived and died on this particular spot." He pointed around. "This building dates back to 1852. It saw the Civil War. The waves of immigrants. The fires, the blizzards and hurricanes, the diseases . . ."

"Diseases?" Eliza echoed.

"Oh, yes," said Mr. Carroll. "Cholera. Polio. Influenza. They cut through the city like pruning shears."

"*Win.*" Mrs. Carroll gave her husband another smack. "You'll give our guests nightmares."

"Oh, ghosts can't hurt anyone," Eliza protested. "Even poltergeists—the most troublesome type of ghost—just break plates and rattle doorknobs and stuff like that."

"Well, it will give *me* nightmares if I think we haven't given you a decent meal after your long day. More brownies?" Mrs. Carroll held out the plate.

"So," Eliza asked, through a mouthful of chocolate, "have you noticed any supernatural activity here?"

Mr. Carroll tugged softly at his beard. "In the shop, no. But up on the fourth floor . . ." He paused, his eyes lingering somewhere above Eliza's head. "Maybe."

Eliza perked up. The *fourth* floor?

Mrs. Carroll sighed loudly and began clearing the plates.

"What's on the fourth floor?" Eliza asked.

"A mess," said Mrs. Carroll, from the kitchen.

Mr. Carroll chuckled. "The attic. And she's right. It is a mess. Full of junk that's been there for decades and that I don't move because it's always been there. And because I'm lazy." He gave Eliza a grin. "But the last time I was up there—and it was *years* ago—I was in a corner, digging through some boxes . . ." His words slowed and softened. "And I swear I heard a voice."

Eliza leaned forward. "What did it say?"

"It sounded like a name." Mr. Carroll frowned. "Like the voice was calling for someone."

"You probably heard someone on the street outside," said Eliza's mother reasonably.

Eliza ignored this. She'd heard something from the attic, too. She knew it. "Did you answer the voice?"

"I don't believe I did." Mr. Carroll narrowed his eyes, remembering. "But I turned around, and for just a second, I could see somebody standing there. Somebody in a hat and dark clothes. Then I stepped closer, and it was gone." His booming voice was nearly a whisper. "Maybe it was just a shadow. But I don't know what could have cast a shadow like *that*."

"And *this* is why I can't take this man camping," said Mrs. Carroll, putting her hands playfully around Mr. Carroll's neck. "The last time the whole family went up to the Catskills, Win had all the kids sitting around the fire, telling them ghost stories, until half of them were screaming. His sister Marcelline had to drive her kids to the nearest motel so they could sleep with the lights on!"

Eliza's mother laughed. So did Mrs. Carroll, and so did Mr. Carroll, so loudly that the glasses on the table jiggled. Tommy took his plate to the sink.

Eliza would have liked to ask a hundred investigative questions. Had Mr. Carroll felt the temperature in the attic change? Had the lights flickered? Had any objects mysteriously moved?

But the conversation had already traveled on, and her mother was telling the story about the camping trip when Eliza had made herself a crown of burrs, and soon the grown-ups were all laughing about other camping disasters, and in a little while, everyone was saying good night.

"I know you, and I know what you're thinking," said her mother, as soon as she and Eliza were headed up the creaky flight of stairs. "You're thinking about exploring that attic."

That was *exactly* what Eliza had been thinking. "No I wasn't," she said. "I was thinking, where does a name like *Moggie* come from?"

"I don't want you going up there on your own," said her mother. "In an old building like this, it might not be safe."

They reached the top of the steps and turned into the third-floor hallway. Two dim electric candles flickered in an old wall sconce. Eliza kept her eye on the candles as they walked past, but the flicker was too regular to be ghost-related. Probably just old wiring. Eliza sagged slightly.

"Do you hear me?" asked her mother, opening the door.

"Yes," said Eliza.

She did hear. She didn't necessarily agree with what she heard—but her mother hadn't asked *that* question.

Her mother flicked on the chandelier. "The Carrolls are nice, aren't they?" she asked, once the door was shut again. "A little flaky, maybe." She started to smile. "Mrs. Carroll and her singing flowers. Mr. Carroll and his mysterious voices. But nice."

"Yes," said Eliza. "Really nice."

"I'm going to see if your father sent an email today." Her mother bent over the table, turning on her laptop. "Would you like first dibs on the shower, sweet pea?"

"I think I'll wait until morning," said Eliza. Figuring out a brand-new shower—which tap did what, and how far to turn each one to keep from scalding or freezing yourself—sounded too tiring. She flopped down onto her creaky bed and pulled out her tablet.

There were no messages from Xavier or Chloe. She hadn't expected there to be. Still, a trickle of disappointment seeped through her chest and dribbled down into her toes.

Xavier and Chloe and Eliza had been best friends since they'd met in the third grade. They'd all loved ghost stories. They'd watched *Ghost Hunters* and *Ghostbusters* and *The Canterville Ghost* together over and over. They'd used Ouija boards and played "Bloody Mary" in the mirror. They'd even snuck out one night to explore the old schoolhouse, which everybody said was haunted.

But over the last few months, Xavier had become more

interested in underground hip-hop and kung fu movies than ghost hunting. And Chloe had become interested in Xavier.

This left Eliza on her own.

Eliza wasn't going to give up her research, though. *She* wasn't going to change.

She switched off the tablet and pulled out her research notebook.

She flipped to a fresh page. At the top, she wrote:

Carrolls' Gardens, New York City

Below that, in careful columns, she recorded all the evidence she'd gathered so far.

> *June 10. ES (Eliza Stahl). Potential ghost sighting: dark figure in front of shop. Approx. 2:00 p.m.*
>
> *June 10. ES. Potential ghost activity (creaking sound): attic. Approx. 2:30 p.m.*
>
> *June 10. ES. Potential ghost sighting: shadow in backyard, behind greenhouse (possibly just dog). Approx. 4:00 p.m.*
>
> *Date? Years ago. WC (Winston Carroll). Potential ghost sighting and hearing: attic.*

Writing down the facts made her heart lift. Four items in one day was a good start. And she was writing in a room that looked like something straight out of a Victorian ghost story. If she returned to Worcester with stories about the spirits she'd encountered in a towering old building in the city, Chloe and Xavier would want to hear every detail. She could picture them sitting on the couch in her basement, just like they used to, poring over her notebooks, hanging on her every word.

Eliza closed the notebook and set it aside.

After putting on her usual pajamas—fuzzy sweatpants and a Sleepy Hollow T-shirt—she climbed under the patchwork quilt.

Nothing about this bed felt right. The squeak of the springs, the texture of the sheets, the shape of the pillow under her head. It was all *different*. Eliza was willing to deal with *different* if it brought her closer to actual ghosts, but it wasn't going to be easy. The smells in the air were the most different part of all: dust and old wood and faint whiffs of plants, beneath a trace of jollof rice. Plus the Carrolls obviously used a different brand of laundry detergent.

Eliza rolled over so she was smelling the sleeve of her own shirt instead. She closed her eyes. The high-ceilinged room disappeared. The sounds of city traffic faded into the background, half-hidden behind the tapping of her mother's fingers on the computer keys. At least *that* sound was familiar.

With the soft clicking in her ears, Eliza finally settled down to rest.

BUT SHE COULDN'T SLEEP.

The differentness of this place was too strong. And the paranormal evidence she'd already collected kept poking her like a bunch of spectral fingers. The fingers poked harder as her mother closed the computer, turned out the light, and climbed into bed. The room settled into silence.

Finally, when she was sure her mother was asleep—and she couldn't stand the poking anymore—Eliza sat up.

The summer sky through the windows had turned to smoky black. A few streetlamps glowed outside, giving just enough light to outline the unfamiliar room. Eliza wriggled toward the side of the bed and touched the power button on her tablet. 12:32. Just after midnight: prime ghost-spotting time.

She swung her feet out of bed. The springs squeaked fussily beneath her, but her mother didn't stir. Eliza tiptoed across the room, trying to avoid any furniture waiting to stub her toes or surprise creaky spots in the floor, into the corner where she'd left her box of ghost things.

She pulled out a candle in a tall glass jar, a book of matches, and her pocket-sized digital thermometer. Then she pushed the stack of books aside and reached to the very bottom, where her fingers closed around a familiar cardboard square.

Last summer, she and Xavier and Chloe had made a ghost-hunting expedition to the woods at Hadwen Park. They'd discussed bringing the Ouija board along for ghost communication, but Ouija boards and bumpy forest paths didn't mix. You couldn't be sure your own steps weren't shoving the planchette around.

So they'd invented their own communication device instead.

Taking the spinner from an old Twister game, they'd covered the cardboard base with fresh paper. They had written YES and NO on the paper, along with the alphabet and four faces with different expressions. To send a message, a ghost just had to tap the spinner.

Chloe had wanted to name their device the Spook Speaker, but Eliza had insisted on calling it the Spectral Translator. It seemed more scientific.

Now, clutching her tools, Eliza tiptoed out the door. The hallway was dark as wet ink. She lit the candle, and its flame pulled one small patch of hallway up out of the blackness. Eliza never brought a flashlight on a ghost-hunting trip.

Ghosts disliked flashlights; their beams were too aggressive. Ghosts' preferences were darkness, moonlight, and candlelight, in that order.

Eliza pulled the door shut behind her. The hallway's wooden floor groaned under her socks. Holding the Translator and the candle out before her, she padded down the hall. The temperature of the air seemed stable: no cold patches, no sudden breezes on the back of her neck. The candle's flame bobbled softly. If a candle burned blue, it meant that spirits were present—but the flame stayed disappointingly orange.

Eliza reached the hall's first door. Tucking the Translator under one arm, she turned the rusty knob and inched the door open. Inside was a small, empty room. By candlelight, she could make out scuffed floorboards, bare rafters, and the edge of a fire escape running past the dirty window. The flame of the candle burned steadily. Eliza shut the door and moved on.

Behind the next door was an ancient laundry room, as boringly ghost-less as the first.

Eliza crept toward the third and final door. Before she had even reached it, she felt a strange sensation, like cool, damp air swirling against her bare ankles. The flame in the candle wobbled. Was she imagining it, or did it look a tiny bit bluish? Eliza grasped the doorknob. It didn't budge.

This had to be the entrance to the attic. And it was the only door that was locked.

Eliza held the Spectral Translator close to the door. No movement. But as she waited, holding her breath, she caught something else.

A soft, shuffling sound. Like footsteps. And it came from above.

Eliza froze.

Yes. There it was again.

A creak. A step. Something was moving in the attic.

Eliza pressed her ear to the cold wood of the door.

There were no voices, but she heard a thump, a click, and a creak. Another damp gust slid over her ankles.

She had to get into the attic.

If she could just slip down to the shop and get the key from its hook behind the counter, and then sneak back upstairs and unlock the door without her mother or the Carrolls hearing her. . . .

Eliza whirled back toward the hallway. But something blocked her path. Something as black as the shadows surrounding it.

Eliza didn't even notice it was there until its bulk struck the front of her legs, sending her and her candle face-first to the floor. She landed with an un-sneaky *thud*. The flame of the candle winked out.

Darkness poured back, blacker than before. And in the darkness, something moved. Something that creaked closer to her. Something with wet, cold breath. Breath that smelled like . . . chicken.

Dim electric light filled the hallway.

Eliza squinted through the light into a pair of gold eyes in a grizzled gray face. Moggie sat before her, panting happily.

"Eliza?" hissed a voice.

Eliza turned.

Her mother stood in the doorway of their room, her hand on the hallway light switch.

"Eliza," she stage-whispered. "What are you *doing*?"

49

Eliza stuffed the Spectral Translator and the candle under her backside. "I heard something, and I came out to see what it was," she said innocently. "I guess it was the dog."

Moggie licked Eliza's chin with a chicken-scented tongue.

"You came out *to see*," her mother repeated. "In *the dark*."

Eliza nudged Moggie away before her chin could get any wetter. "Yep."

"You didn't sneak out here planning to do some ghost hunting in the attic, immediately after I'd told you not to."

Moggie licked Eliza's ear. Eliza wiped it on her shoulder. "Nope."

"I'm glad to hear it," said her mother. "Now, get back in here and into your bed before you wake up the rest of the building, please." She turned sideways, gesturing for Eliza to step through the door.

Eliza clambered to her feet. Keeping the candle and the Spectral Translator behind her, she sidled past her mother into their borrowed room. Her mother switched off the hall light and closed the door.

Eliza didn't get to throw a last glance at the locked attic or at Moggie sitting guard outside it. But the scene lingered in her mind, clear enough to touch.

After they had both gone back to bed, and her mother was breathing deeply beside her, Eliza rolled over and grabbed her research notebook.

July 11, she wrote, squinting through the dimness.

Possible ghost activity: attic. Creaking sounds.
Footsteps? 1:00 a.m. Need to find out more.

And she would.

Eliza closed the notebook and flopped back in bed. Then, staring up at the high gray ceiling, she started to smile.

Something spooky is definitely happening here. Good thing Eliza is on the case! Turn to page 209.

THE NEXT DAY WAS a busy one at Carrolls' Gardens. Shoppers filled the store all morning, keeping Mr. Carroll chatting in the main room and Mrs. Carroll fluttering in the floral department. Eliza's mother burrowed down in the workroom, open books piled around her like stacks of paper pancakes, muttering to herself about crenate and crenulate leaves.

Even Eliza was too busy to think about the attic. The Carrolls gave Eliza her very own Carrolls' Gardens name tag, which made her an official store employee. Mrs. Carroll taught her how to help customers. She was supposed to ask "Can I help you find anything?" and, unless the customers' answer was "The bathroom," to send them straight to someone else.

When she wasn't pointing customers to one of those two places, she was helping Tommy with chores. They wiped the front windows. They put away a shipment of water picks and floral wire. In the late morning, they headed into the leafy depths of the rare-plant room.

Tommy mumbled something about picking up any dead leaves. Then he turned around and stumbled over the laces of his own shoes.

Eliza bent to pick up some broken palm fronds. From the corner of her eye, she glanced at Tommy. He was dusting leaves with a soft white cloth. Tommy looked even more slumped and saggy this morning, Eliza thought. He looked . . . tired. Could her tripping over Moggie have woken him in the middle of the night? Or—maybe—could he have heard the sounds coming from the attic, too? Did he know something important about the place, something she just hadn't thought to ask? Eliza's breath caught. Maybe she could—

"Look out!" said Tommy.

Eliza jerked upright. Her head bumped something that squished. Sticky wetness dribbled along her neck and into the collar of her T-shirt. Eliza looked above her. She'd straightened up right beneath a hanging basket, where a plant with long, sleek leaves and flowers like streaky pink genie bottles was swaying wildly back and forth.

Eliza swiped at her neck. "What is it? Is it poison? Am I dead?"

Tommy stepped toward her. "It's okay," he mumbled. He patted the damp spot on her shoulder with his cloth. "It's just sappy stuff. The plant uses it to lure bugs." He squinted down at her shirt. "At least there weren't any dead bugs in that one."

Eliza checked her shoulder. Tommy was right: no dead bugs. That was a plus.

"It's a pitcher plant," Tommy explained, wiping a streak on her neck. "They're carnivorous."

Eliza perked up. "Carnivorous?"

"They're bug-eating. Not, like, *man*-eating." In the middle of another wipe, Tommy seemed to realize that he was touching a girl. He backed rapidly away, leaving Eliza to grab the rag on her shoulder. "They only eat insects," he said, shaking his hair back over his eyes. "They dissolve them and absorb them. Like Venus flytraps do."

Eliza threw another look at the plant. Its pink-green pitchers bobbled tauntingly.

Embarrassment seemed to have knocked Tommy's words loose. "People usually call them pitcher plants, because of how they're shaped," he hurried on. "Or monkey cups, because monkeys like to drink that sticky stuff, too. But their real name is *Nepenthes*."

"*Nepenthes?*" Eliza instantly forgot the sticky stuff on her neck. "Like in 'The Raven' by Edgar Allan Poe? 'Respite and nepenthe from thy memories of Lenore'?"

"Um. I guess." Tommy blinked at her. "They get used in painkillers. *Nepenthe* means 'without grief.'"

Eliza stared at Tommy. All at once, she felt solid—like

for the first time since arriving at Carrolls' Gardens, both her feet were planted on the floor. "You know weird stuff," she told him.

Tommy looked like he'd just been sloshed by a pitcher plant of his own. He gave a startled twitch. Then he fixed his eyes on the floor, taking two shuffling steps backward.

"That's *good*," said Eliza, before Tommy could shuffle straight out of the room. She smiled. "I know weird stuff, too. I mean—I just quoted 'The Raven' at you."

Tommy stopped shuffling. "Oh." He gave Eliza a glance from under the shaggy ends of his hair. She couldn't tell if he was smiling back, but he might have been.

"So, you really think this plant stuff is interesting?" Eliza gazed around at the twining vines and gleaming berries and the flowers shaped like tropical birds. *"Why?"*

"Um ..." Tommy scratched his head with one hand, making his hair hang even more crookedly. "What you said about ghost research the other night—that's kind of like plant science. You know, witches putting a bunch of weird herbs in a pot, making potions, figuring out plants' powers. It sounds like magic. But that's how *medicine* began." He nodded around the leafy room. "Plants are science *and* magic."

"Science and magic," Eliza repeated. She stuffed the damp rag into her pocket. "Have you ever read the story 'Rappaccini's Daughter'?"

Tommy shook his head.

"It's about this obsessive botanist guy who feeds his daughter little bits of poisonous plants." Eliza dropped her voice to a spooky storytelling register. "He gives her more and more over time, so eventually she's not just immune to all the poisons, she *becomes poisonous*. Like, she can kill people if she touches them. Or even breathes on them. It's supposed to just be this creepy story. But I suppose it could actually be *true*."

Tommy's hazel eyes grew wider. "Cool," he breathed.

Eliza was used to most people *not* thinking "Rappaccini's Daughter" was cool. She beamed at Tommy. She was about to launch into another creepy story—maybe "The Willows"—when Tommy whirled around.

"I'll show you something," he called over his shoulder.

Eliza followed him through the leaves to a shrub with glossy black berries.

"This is belladonna," said Tommy. "A super-famous poison. Also known as deadly nightshade."

Eliza had heard the name *deadly nightshade* in plenty of stories. She stared down at the plant. Its berries were beautiful, like little drops of blackberry jam. "You sell poisonous plants here?"

"Tons of normal houseplants are poisonous," Tommy pointed out. "Peace lilies. Narcissus. Dieffenbachia. Philodendrons are really poisonous, and everybody's got one of them in their living room." He crouched beside the plants.

"Just a couple belladonna berries can kill a little kid. But people have also used it in medicine, or built up a tolerance to it—like that Rappahannock's Daughter girl—"

"Rappaccini's."

"Right. People have even made the berries' juice into wine. *Poison* wine." Tommy touched a jet-black berry with one fingertip. His voice was smooth and confident now, not mumbly at all. "There are legends of ancient kings killing entire enemy armies by tricking them with gifts of bella donna wine."

"Wow," said Eliza. The words *poison wine* sent a pleasant shiver rippling up her back. "You make plants actually sound interesting."

Tommy flushed. He smiled down at the floor. "They *are* interesting. I mean, I think they are."

"You know who you should hang out with? My mom."

Tommy's eyes widened. "Oh. I wouldn't want to bother her. . . ."

"You won't. She *loves* having somebody to talk to about this stuff. In the summers, when she doesn't have her classes to teach, it usually ends up being *me*. Come on."

They found her mother at the workroom table, scalpel in hand, bending over something in a metal tray. Beside her was the plant with the golden leaves and bright red berries. As Eliza moved closer, with Tommy trailing after her, she saw that the tray held one of those berries, neatly sliced in half.

"Hello, you two." Her mother glanced up. She nodded at Eliza's wet shoulder. "Did Moggie get you again?"

"It was *Nepenthes* this time." Eliza leaned against the worktable. "We just thought we'd come and see how things are going."

"Oh, they're going!" Her mother started to poke the scalpel into the bun on top of her head, but stopped herself just in time. "I'm getting a good look at this berry. It's similar to a red currant, really, in texture and in color. But the epicarp—its skin—is tougher. And you can see the seeds, right here . . ." She pointed with the scalpel. Tommy leaned in eagerly. "The seeds aren't like those in a currant or a grape. They're closer to a blueberry's."

"Hmm," said Tommy. "So . . . um . . . do you think it's edible?"

"Hard to say. Without eating it, that is." Her mother pressed the tip of the scalpel against her open notebook, then put the scalpel down and grabbed a pencil from her bun. She scribbled a few words. "It could be edible. It could have medicinal properties. It could be toxic, although it's not contact-poisonous. I've tested it on my skin already." She tapped her cheek dreamily with the pencil's eraser. Eliza reached out and pulled the scalpel out of her mother's reach. "I'm sure your aunt and uncle wouldn't love the idea of rodents in the shop, but if I could have just a couple of mice . . ."

"Mice?" echoed Eliza.

"Animals' senses of smell are far more developed than ours. If a mouse willingly ate the berry and *survived*, then—" Her mother broke off with a sigh. "No. Never mind. A few weeks isn't enough time for animal studies anyway." She lifted the berry to her nose and sniffed.

Eliza grabbed her mother's wrist. "Mom, you're not going to *eat* that, are you?"

"No," said her mother. "I'm just smelling it." She took another sniff. "Sweet. Slightly tangy. One would think it had evolved to attract potential eaters, who would then distribute its seeds through excretion. Smell?" She held it out on her palm.

Tommy craned in and took an avid sniff. The word *excretion*—which Eliza knew was scientist-speak for *poo*— made her not-so-interested in sniffing anything, but she finally leaned toward the berry and inhaled, too.

The fruit *did* smell sweet. Kind of like a cranberry candle. But Eliza didn't care much about cranberry candles or rare red-berried plants. Tommy, on the other hand, looked like he'd never seen anything more fascinating than this bisected berry.

"Um . . . would a plant maybe evolve to *seem* edible but actually be poisonous?" he asked.

"Good question!" Her mother smiled. "Many poisonous plants do have edible lookalikes: wild grapes and *Menispermum canadense*, chestnut and *Aesculus* or buckeye . . ."

Her mother went on, using terms like *Vavilovian mimicry* and *phytochemistry*, making gestures that got bigger and bigger. Tommy listened, his face intent. Eliza's mind began to feel like a salad spinner, full of leafy green words that she couldn't quite grasp.

She took a step toward the door. "Well—I'm going to finish picking up in the rare plant room."

Tommy jerked. "Oh. Yeah. I should go, too."

"No." Eliza waved a hand. "I'll do it. You two keep talking about buckeye excretions or whatever. Have fun."

Tommy gave a shy smile.

Eliza stepped out the door, smiling, too. She'd done something nice for Tommy. That felt good. Of course, it didn't get her any closer to uncovering the ghostly mysteries of this place, but—

Wait.

Maybe it would.

Eliza scanned the shop.

Mr. Carroll was carrying a customer's crate of plants toward the front door. "I'll load up these orchids for you," he told her. "Of course, it will cost you extra." He boomed a big laugh. "Just orchid-ing!" The bell jingled as they stepped outside.

Mrs. Carroll's voice fluted out from the floral department. "What was that, *Ranunculus*, dear? These mums are drowning you out. Sing out! You've got such a lovely voice!"

Eliza slipped across the room and circled behind the counter. With the attic key, she'd dash upstairs, unlock the

door, and return the key to its hook. Then she could explore the attic at her leisure later tonight.

She reached for the ATTIC hook.

It was empty.

Eliza frowned. She crouched to check the floor. Maybe the key had fallen somewhere nearby. She was hunched there, groping around, when a voice said—

"Excuse me?"

Eliza looked up.

A woman with sleek black hair stood at the counter. "Do you carry seaweed fertilizer?"

"Like . . . for growing seaweed?" Eliza asked.

The woman blinked. "No. It's made of seaweed. Kelp. *Laminaria.* Bladder wrack. Do you have any?"

"Um . . ." Eliza glanced around the shop. Mr. Carroll hadn't come back inside. Mrs. Carroll was still giving her flowers a pep talk. Tommy was shut in the workroom. Well, Eliza could handle this on her own. Tommy had told her where they kept the fertilizer.

"Let me check the basement," she told the woman. She pulled the BASEMENT key from its hook. "I'll be right back."

She hurried through the rare plant room into the hallway.

The basement door opened with one turn of the key. Eliza patted the inner walls until she found a light switch. Somewhere below, a dim gold light blinked on.

Eliza gazed down the stairs. They were steep and wooden, with railings blocking the emptiness on either side. The basement itself—as much of it as she could glimpse—had brick walls and a cement floor. It was filled with the kind of darkness that told Eliza the light she'd turned on was probably one bare, hanging bulb.

Eliza pattered down the stairs. The air against her skin grew cooler. The smell of soil gusted around her, mixed with a whiff of chemicals or mold or something else she couldn't recognize. She reached the bare stone floor and took a look around.

This basement wasn't so different from the basements in most old houses. She could make out the metal tanks of appliances, the twining pipes climbing up the walls and across the ceiling like big bare veins. Shelves piled with sacks and crates and boxes—boxes that Eliza hoped contained seaweed fertilizer—stood all around. A breeze whispered over the back of her neck.

Wait.

Where was a breeze coming from?

Eliza glanced over her shoulder. Was there an open window down here? No—there couldn't be, not so far underground.

The hairs on her neck rose. This breeze wasn't a dog's breath. This breeze had to be something else. Something *supernatural*. Wishing she had her thermometer or her

Spectral Translator along, Eliza turned toward the basement's depths.

Another touch of cold air brushed her skin. It was coming from the darkness behind the stairs. Eliza's skin tingled. The darkness itself seemed to be calling her to come closer, closer, closer—

"What are you doing?"

Eliza whirled around.

Tommy stood at the bottom of the stairs. Half hidden by dimness and shaggy hair, his face was hard to read—but it was definitely not smiling.

Eliza's heart thudded in her throat like a tiny basketball. "I was just looking for something."

Tommy stared down at her. "For what?"

"A customer wanted seaweed fertilizer. You said you kept fertilizer down here, so . . ." Tommy's gaze flicked past her into the shadows. There was no sound but the rumbling of the pipes.

"I'll get it," he said at last. "You should go upstairs. My aunt and uncle don't want anybody down here."

"Why not?"

Tommy looked straight at her now. "Because it's not safe."

This could have meant many different things. Eliza would have liked to find out which one it *did* mean, but something in Tommy's voice halted her. Sometimes his voice was mumbly; sometimes it was smooth and clear and enthusiastic. Now it was smooth but *cold*. And very hard. It was a lot like the chilly stone underneath her shoes.

"Okay," said Eliza. "Sorry."

She moved past him, up the steps.

"Wait."

Eliza halted. Maybe Tommy was going to explain something about the basement. Maybe he'd decided he could trust her. She turned to him, hopeful.

But all he said was "The key." He held out his hand.

Eliza dropped the basement key into his palm. Then she hurried up the stairs.

Tommy didn't speak to her for the rest of the day. They continued silently with their chores, working on the opposite sides of each room.

Tension spread through Eliza's body. Her head felt tight. Her back ached. She stretched it while dusting the leaves of rubber plants. Her stomach ached, too, but she couldn't stretch that. She'd started to feel not quite *friendly* with Tommy, but something friendly-ish. It had been nice to talk to someone who wanted to listen, who had odd hobbies of his own, who even knew what the word *Nepenthe* meant. She'd started to hope that he would help with her Carrolls' Gardens ghost hunting—because clearly, there were ghosts here to be hunted. But now everything had changed. And this time the change was her own fault.

She glanced over at Tommy just once, while they were

both checking for weeds in the greenhouse flats. She found him looking straight back at her. His hazel eyes were icy. And for once, Eliza was the first one to look away.

AWKWARD!
Is this going to put the brakes on Eliza's explorations? Or is it going to make her SURE that there's something here to investigate?
Turn to page 225.

8

WHEN ELIZA WOKE IN the middle of that night, it wasn't a coincidence.

She'd set her tablet to vibrate at 12:30 and slipped it underneath her pillow. But as it turned out, it wasn't vibration that woke her. It was a crash of thunder.

Eliza jerked backward in bed. A flash of lightning bleached the turret windows. Rain hissed against the panes. She pulled out her tablet. 12:24. She hadn't even needed to set the alarm.

Another smash of thunder shook the big brick building. The windows rattled. Raindrops pounded on the turret's metal roof. In the other bed, her mother didn't stir.

Eliza slipped out of the covers and darted across the room to the turret. The cushions of the encircling window seat were covered in threadbare velvet, like the seats in an old movie theater. Eliza knelt on the seat and pressed her face to the window. If she pressed hard enough and looked straight down, she could see the windows of the Carrolls' apartment, as well as the shop below. All the lights were out. Except for the headlights of a rusty pickup truck coasting along the pavement, the entire street was dark.

This was her chance.

With the Spectral Translator in hand, Eliza raced out into the hall, down both flights of stairs, and into the deserted store.

By night, Carrolls' Gardens looked even more like a patch of strange forest. Fronds and stems twisted through the dark. Flickers of lightning turned each plant to layers of black paper silhouettes. It was impossible to tell what was real and what was only a shadow.

Dodging the fluttering leaves, Eliza made her way to the counter. She reached for the spare keys.

Now the hook labeled BASEMENT was empty.

Something more like frustration than surprise whooshed through her. First the attic, and now the basement? Tommy must have decided to hide the key, to keep her from getting into the basement again. Well, that wasn't going to stop her. Maybe she could remove the doorknob with a screwdriver; the greenhouse must have a few tools that could help. Maybe she could even pick the lock. The noise of the storm would provide the perfect cover.

With the Spectral Translator in one hand and a lock-picking paperclip from the counter drawers in her pocket, Eliza threaded through the rare plant room, avoiding thorns and stingers and sticky leaves. Fronds whispered around her. Thunder boomed, shaking the walls.

In the back hallway, hard rain spattered the windows. But now, beneath the noise, Eliza heard something else.

Voices.

Eliza halted.

Two voices. Men's voices. One deep. One raspy and soft.

A flash of lightning bleached the hallway. By its light, Eliza could see that the basement door was standing wide open.

She rolled her head from side to side. She stretched both wrists. Then, her whole body zinging and ready, she inched closer to the open door.

Cold, wet air swirled up from below.

One of the voices spoke again. Eliza couldn't make out its words. Could this be the same voice Mr. Carroll had heard in the attic years ago? Or were multiple ghosts haunting the rooms of Carrolls' Gardens, just waiting for Eliza to discover them?

She tiptoed down the first two steps. She had expected the basement to be blindingly dark—but instead, from somewhere out of sight, there came a dim glow. What was going on down here?

With slightly shaky hands, Eliza held out the Translator. The spinner wobbled, stopping just above the angry face—but it could have been the breeze or her shaking that moved it.

She crept down the steps. The chill of the stone floor seeped through her socks like ice water. As Eliza hesitated, trying to trace the source of the breeze, a voice spoke.

And this time, Eliza recognized it.

"Any more?" said Mr. Carroll's deep voice.

"A few," rasped the other.

Eliza held her breath. Was Mr. Carroll speaking to the ghost?

She slunk past a sagging wooden shelf. Around its edge, she made out a burning lightbulb in a dirty glass fixture. Beside the light was a gap in the basement's stone wall—a gap filled with another flight of stairs.

Eliza crept closer. More of the staircase slid into view. The steps led steeply upward, their wooden slats dripping with rain. At the top of the steps, Eliza could see an open cellar door leading out to the stormy backyard. And standing on the staircase, his back to her, was the broad, dark shape of Mr. Carroll.

Eliza halted again, her mind whirling. Was *this* the cold spot? Just a draft from an open doorway? And what was Mr. Carroll doing in it? She inched nearer. Damp wind struck her face, lifting the ends of her hair.

Mr. Carroll waited on the stairs. Rain pattered around him. As Eliza watched, a second figure—something dressed in a battered sweater and knit cap—appeared at the very top of the steps. Eliza couldn't make out its face, but it looked too solid to be a ghost. Its tattoo-covered hands passed Mr. Carroll a bundle.

"That one's heavy," said the raspy voice. "Two more."

"All right," Mr. Carroll murmured back.

The other figure disappeared.

Mr. Carroll thumped down the steps. He set the bundle on the floor in a line of other bundles. Eliza squinted at them. The bundles varied widely in size, but each one was wrapped in burlap and shaped like a lumpy hourglass. Sticking out here and there through gaps in the fabric were bits of green.

Twigs. Leaves.

The bundles were full of plants.

For an instant, Eliza felt furious. She'd expected to find a ghost at last. Instead, she'd found a bunch of *shrubs*?

She let out a long, hot breath through her nose. She was about to turn away when a new thought plunged into her brain.

What kind of plants did people hand off at midnight, in a rainstorm, through a hidden basement door?

Eliza stopped.

Dangerous plants. Poisons. Drugs. Or something even worse. Frost spread through her body, fizzling the anger away. What kind of secret had she stumbled into?

This was the trouble with people. They had complicated, messy, confusing problems. She was interested in ghosts, not in real life. Whatever was happening here, with the Carrolls and the raspy-voiced stranger and the bundled plants, it wasn't the kind of thing that belonged in Eliza's paranormal research notebook. It didn't belong there—and she didn't belong *here*.

With her heart jammed in her windpipe, Eliza raced back toward the stairs. She climbed as carefully and quietly as she could, away from the dim gold basement light and deeper into the stormy blackness. By the time she reached the upper hall, her legs were shaking, and the darkness was so thick she was nearly blind.

She stopped for a moment in the hall, gasping, holding out a hand to make sure the path around her was clear. Another bolt of lightning flashed. It illuminated the deserted greenhouse and the rain-soaked backyard. It filled the hallway windows with white light. It flared on the face pressed against one of those windows—the face of some-one, or some*thing*, waiting in the rainy yard. Something dark and hunched. Something cloaked in black.

Something that stared straight back at Eliza with a pair of blazing yellow eyes.

It didn't matter how quietly she had climbed the base-ment steps.

Because now Eliza let out a quiet-shattering scream.

AAAAAAAAAAIIIIIIIIIIIEEEEEEEE!
Turn to page 231.

ELIZA SLAPPED A HAND over her mouth.

But it was too late.

The sound of footsteps echoed up from the basement. Meanwhile, in the backyard, the yellow eyes had disappeared. Whatever they belonged to had backed away and dwindled into the night.

Heavy feet clomped up the basement staircase.

Eliza threw herself into the rare plant room and dived behind a giant palm. The shadows around her swayed.

The footsteps creaked closer.

Eliza's lungs squeezed into two hard, breathless knots.

Through the dark slashes of the palm fronds, she watched Mr. Carroll step from the hallway into the rare plant room. Even in the dimness, she could see the glitter of raindrops on his Hawaiian shirt. She hunched as low as she could, praying that another flash of lightning wouldn't burn through the shadows and give her away.

Mr. Carroll stopped a few feet from her hiding spot. His usually jolly face was wary. His dark eyes glinted as they scanned the room. For the first time, Eliza realized not just how big and broad, but how *intimidating* Mr. Carroll was. He looked like someone who wouldn't be afraid to confront an intruder with nothing but his bare hands.

Maybe she should step out from behind the potted palm right now. She could explain that she had been ghost hunting and gotten scared, and Mr. Carroll would probably laugh his big laugh and tell her he'd keep an eye out for any ghosts, and then they would probably both head up to bed, pretending nothing strange had happened. But something in Mr. Carroll's face kept her stuck to the wall. Something hard and cold. Something she hadn't seen there before. It reminded her of Tommy's cold, hard voice. Were *both* of them keeping secrets?

As Eliza shivered, holding her breath tight, Mr. Carroll slowly turned back toward the hallway. His heavy footsteps creaked away. There was the thud of the closing basement door.

Eliza flew out from behind the potted palm.

She tore up both flights of stairs and down the dark hallway into her room.

Her mother was still in bed, sleeping soundly.

Dropping her ghost-hunting tools, Eliza leaped into her own bed. She lay there like uncooked spaghetti.

Minutes ticked by. Eliza stretched everything she could

stretch while lying down: her ankles, her hands, her hamstrings.

Finally, no closer to relaxing, Eliza slid out of bed, crept to her box, and grabbed her research notebook.

She made her way to the turret in the corner. The storm was fading to a softer rainfall now. Just enough light misted up from the streetlamps for her to see the pages.

Eliza reread her list: her careful notes about the sighting on the street, the sounds in the basement, the story of the attic.

July 13, 12:30–1:30 a.m., she added. *Possible ghost sighting: Backyard of Carrolls' Gardens. Dark figure. Yellow eyes.* And then, even though it *didn't* belong with her paranormal research, she wrote:

> *Mysterious activity: Basement. Mr. C. speaking to unknown person (?) at hidden back door. Handing off plants. WHY?*

Eliza closed the notebook.

Usually ghost hunting made her feel electrified and happy—but now she felt electrified and jittery, like the energy coursing through her was the wrong voltage, and it could start to burn.

There was at least one mystery haunting this place. There was a spectral presence—no human being had eyes that yellow color—and there was the mystery of Mr. Carroll and the basement plants. Maybe the two were connected somehow. The yellow eyes had appeared right after she'd witnessed the weirdness in the basement. . . .

If only she had someone to talk to about all of this. Eliza was used to most people not believing in the value of psychical research, but now, without Chloe or Xavier, and with Tommy not speaking to her, she was entirely alone.

Eliza took a breath.

Well—then she would do this alone.

She would find answers. She would keep searching.

Eliza slipped down from the window seat and padded back across the room. If she had stayed for just a moment longer, she would have seen a final weak flash of lightning illuminate the street. She would have seen it glancing off the pavement, turning puddles to mirrors and leaves to flickering tinsel. She would have seen a large, hunched figure gliding away from Carrolls' Gardens, slipping into the shadows just as the light faded.

But Eliza had already climbed into bed.

And the dark figure had disappeared once more.

BY THE TIME ELIZA woke up the next morning, her mother's bed was empty and neatly made. The light streaming through the turret windows was bright. She pulled on some clothes, ate a cold toaster pastry, and hurried down the stairs.

Mrs. Carroll was in the floral department, watering a basket of ivy. "I know you wish you had flowers," Eliza heard her murmuring, "but greenery is just as lovely, and it doesn't fade!" She stopped to flash Eliza a sunny smile. "Good morning, dear!—Now, pay no attention to that bridal veil plant. It's just feeling insecure. . . ."

Eliza headed across the shop.

The door to her mother's workroom was closed. Eliza inched it open and peeped inside. Her mother stood at the central table, the red-berried plant and something with long purplish leaves sitting before her. She was bent over an open book, whispering softly to herself.

Part of Eliza wanted to dart inside, close the door behind her, and tell her mother all about the night before. But that would mean admitting that she'd sneaked out of bed—again—to ghost hunt. And it would mean admitting that she couldn't handle this mystery on her own.

Eliza shut the door.

She turned back toward the shop. The main room glowed with morning sun. Its light filtered through a thousand leaves, turning them to glinting emerald and amber. A few customers examined water lilies in the bubbling indoor pond.

"Good morning, Eliza!" Mr. Carroll boomed from behind the counter. "I hope that storm didn't keep you up all night!"

"Um . . . nope," said Eliza. She shifted in her shoes. "What can I help with?"

"Why don't you take it easy today?" Mr. Carroll suggested. "Find a sunny spot. Read a book. I could bring you a glass of my famous sweet tea." His smile broadened. "It *is* your summer vacation, after all."

Maybe she was imagining it, but Mr. Carroll's smile looked different this morning. It was like something microwaved: warm at the edges, but with a hard frozen spot in the middle. Did he suspect something? He *had* heard her scream. . . .

Eliza swallowed. "That's okay," she managed. "I like to keep busy."

"And I like people who like to keep busy." Mr. Carroll waved a hand the size of a baseball glove. "The greenhouse needs sweeping. You could start there!"

Eliza wound through the rare plant room and into the hall. She checked the window where that shadowy face had pressed itself, its yellow eyes burning in at her—even though she knew there'd be nothing there. Then she pushed through the glass doors into the greenhouse.

Tommy stood at the greenhouse's far end. His shaggy head was bowed over a small table, where a few potted plants and tools and papers were scattered. He didn't look up.

The wide push broom leaned against the outer wall. Eliza grabbed it and began brushing dead leaves and spilled dirt out from under the tables. The broom rasped softly. Tommy still didn't turn.

He must have decided to ignore her completely.

A thought struck Eliza. Did Tommy know about the basement plants? Had he warned her away from the basement in order to keep his uncle—or the mystery—safe? Had he actually been trying to protect Eliza from something? She would have liked to find out, if Tommy hadn't been giving her the silent treatment. Eliza swallowed a lump in her throat. It was strange: Having a friend—or an almost-friend—and then losing him felt worse than never having had a friend at all.

Eliza was just thrusting the broom beneath another table when something let out a loud *Mmmmrrrff!!*

Eliza jumped. The broom hit the floor with a smack.

Groaning lazily, Moggie hauled herself out from under the table. She took her time stretching each back leg, and then her spine, grunting and snuffling all the while. Eliza hoped she didn't look like that when *she* stretched.

She glanced up. Tommy had turned around. He was staring straight at her, his face wary.

"Oh," said Eliza uncertainly.

"Um . . . ," said Tommy even more uncertainly. His fingers twitched toward the tabletop behind him. "I didn't—um—didn't hear you come in."

"Oh," said Eliza again. Maybe he *hadn't* meant to ignore her. "Sorry for startling you."

"It's okay," said Tommy. Without turning his back to Eliza, he angled toward the table and stuffed a couple of papers into his pocket. "I was just . . . concentrating."

"On what?"

"Nothing." Tommy's voice dropped to an unfriendly mumble. "I'll get the dust pan."

"Wait." Eliza spoke up before Tommy could slouch away.

"I wanted to apologize about going into the basement. I was just trying to help. So I hope you won't . . ." Eliza felt her neck growing tenser. She rolled her shoulders back and took a breath. "I hope you won't hate me."

Tommy didn't answer. He just stood, blinking at the floor, while Eliza stretched her head carefully from side to side. Then, with silence still hanging in the air between them, he turned and strode past her, straight out of the greenhouse. Moggie trotted after him.

Eliza's heart plunged. Apparently an apology wasn't enough.

She bent and picked up the broom. She wished she were home, in her own familiar house, in her own familiar room, with all her books and snacks and ghost souvenirs. If she had to be alone, at least she could do it there, where the sheets smelled right. She shoved the broom under the next table. The backs of her eyelids prickled.

She'd just finished sweeping the row when a voice said, "Hey."

Eliza nearly dropped the broom again.

Tommy stood beside her, holding out a potted plant with slender stems and deep blue-purple blossoms. "Monkshood," he said.

"It's pretty," said Eliza.

"Don't touch it!" Tommy warned as she reached out a hand. "Just touching it can make you sick."

"Oh." Eliza stared at Tommy through the cluster of

flowers. Suddenly the pretty plant felt like a live bomb. And Tommy was holding it out between them.

Was he *threatening* her?

Before she could be sure, Tommy blurted, "I read that story. 'Rappaccini's Daughter.'"

Eliza blinked. "You did?"

"Yeah. I found it online."

"Did you like it?"

Tommy shrugged. "It was okay. Kind of old-fashioned and weird. But I liked the stuff about the plants." He nodded down at the plant. "That main flower he described, the beautiful purple one, the one that's poisonous even to touch . . . It made me think of this."

"Oh." The tightness in Eliza's neck loosened. Moggie, who had followed Tommy back into the greenhouse, flopped down with a loud sigh between their feet.

"Its real name is *Aconitum*, but people call it Queen of Poisons, Devil's Helmet, all kinds of stuff," Tommy went on. "A tiny bit of it can kill a person in hours. It's related to wolfsbane—*Aconitum lycoctonum*—which has been used in all kinds of mystery stories. You know that old movie *Dracula*? The black-and-white one?"

Eliza nodded. Before his kung fu movie phase, Xavier had been a classic horror film fan. He and Chloe and Eliza had watched practically everything starring Boris Karloff or Bela Lugosi or Vincent Price. *Tales of Terror* was Eliza's favorite, but *Dracula* had been pretty good, too.

"In *Dracula*, they put wolfsbane wreaths everywhere, to keep the vampires away."

"Oh yeah," said Eliza slowly. "I remember."

Tommy turned the plant so the indigo flowers swayed. He looked back up into Eliza's eyes. "I just thought, because of that story, that you might . . . I don't know," he faltered. "I thought you might think it was interesting."

"Yes," said Eliza before Tommy could look away again. "It *is* like the story. It's really cool." She smiled. "Thanks. Thank you."

Tommy blinked. One side of his mouth rose. "Sure. I mean . . . you're welcome." Then he turned and carried the plant away.

Eliza went on smiling as she swept beneath the next table. Maybe she wasn't completely alone.

"**D**ON'T YOU LOOK *BEAUTIFUL?*" cooed Mrs. Carroll. She wasn't talking to Eliza. She was talking to the box of bouquets in Eliza's hands. "Just put them right in the back of the van, dear," she sang. "Thank you!"

Eliza slid the box into place between two others. Tommy set another box beside it, and Mr. Carroll slammed the van's back door.

"The wedding reception is just a few miles away. Setup shouldn't take long." Mr. Carroll nodded toward the shop glowing in the pinkish afternoon sun. "It's a quiet time of day, and the place is in good hands with you two. And if anyone has any burning botanical issues—and I don't mean poison ivy!" He interrupted himself with a laugh. "Remember that Mrs. Stahl is there to help, too."

"Thank you, dear!" Mrs. Carroll sang again, through the open driver's-side window. "*Both* dears!"

Mr. Carroll climbed into the passenger seat. The Carrolls'

Gardens van, with its painted leaves and swirling vines, whooshed off down the street.

Eliza and Tommy stepped back into the shop.

Mr. Carroll was right; it was a quiet time. Nobody moved among the thick plants except for Moggie, who was moving so slowly it almost didn't count.

"Um . . . as long as no one's here," said Tommy, "would you mind if I go back to my work in the greenhouse?"

"Sure," said Eliza. "Moggie and I can handle things out here."

Moggie sprawled on the floor and sighed.

Tommy disappeared through the rare plant room, leaving Eliza and the snoring dog on their own.

Eliza surveyed the room. Ruddy wisps of late-afternoon sun reached through the windows, softening the shades of green all around. The pond bubbled softly. In the far wall, the door to her mother's workroom was closed.

Eliza stepped behind the cash register counter. Moggie raised her head with a little wheeze.

"Shh," Eliza whispered. "You can keep sleeping."

But Moggie lumbered to her feet. She followed Eliza, her yellow eyes tracking each movement.

Eliza checked the row of hanging keys. Both the attic and the basement keys were still missing.

Eliza sighed. Tommy had obviously taken the basement key. But what about the attic? Was someone using the fourth floor—or trying to keep her out of it?

Eliza stepped slowly out from behind the counter. Moggie waddled after her.

Maybe one of the Carrolls had taken the key, although Eliza couldn't guess why. Or maybe it was someone else. Maybe it was a poltergeist, a restless spirit trying to make trouble or to lead Eliza toward some long-hidden secret that—

The bell above the shop door jingled. Eliza jumped.

A young man and woman in casual clothes breezed inside.

"Welcome to Carrolls' Gardens," said Eliza, in her most grown-up voice. "Is there anything I can help you find?"

The woman smiled. "We're just browsing."

The bell tinkled as someone else stepped inside.

"Great," Eliza told the young couple. "Our most popular plants are here in the main room, and our more unusual items are in the second chamber, just through that archway."

"Thank you very much," said the woman.

Eliza turned away, feeling proud of herself. *Our more unusual items.* Very professional and grown-up.

She scanned the room for the other customer. There was no one among the orchids, or sniffing the blooming perennials, as far as she could see, but the plants were so thick she might have been looking for a bird in a forest. Still, the customer had to be somewhere nearby. Eliza wound through the shelves. To her right, behind a rack of ferns, something gray fluttered.

Eliza stepped around the ferns.

And there he was.

A man in a dark coat and wide-brimmed hat.

His back was to her. He was looking down at a plant, but as Eliza approached, he stiffened. His chin rose. His body went still.

"Hello," said Eliza brightly. "Welcome to Carrolls' Gardens."

The man spun to face her.

His coat was long black wool—so long it almost brushed the floor. Its waist was gathered so that the back flared and pooled around him as he moved. It closed with funny old-fashioned buttons that might have been made of wood or bone. The man's hat was old-fashioned, too; not a top hat or a tricorn, but something broad, made of wool felt.

Between the hat and the coat's high collar, Eliza could hardly see the man's face. What she could glimpse was very pale, almost gray. Even his eyes were hidden, covered by a pair of sunglasses, the cheap plastic kind you find in convenience stores. The sunglasses looked so strange with the man's antique outfit that Eliza did a double take. It was like noticing that someone had added swimming goggles to the *Mona Lisa*. And the whole ensemble—except for the sunglasses—was completely wrong for a sunny summer day. It would almost have been funny . . . except for the way that, from behind those plastic sunglasses, she could feel the man's eyes staring down at her.

As Eliza stood, staring back, everything within the shop seemed to go quiet. A gush of cold washed over her. She could feel it rushing into her nose, down to her lungs, rippling over the rising hairs on her arms. Even time seemed to freeze, the seconds inching by so slowly and strangely that Eliza had no idea how long she had stood there, staring up at the dark-coated man.

But she knew one thing.

This man was no ordinary human being.

He might have been human once. But not anymore.

Eliza took a step backward. She nearly toppled over Moggie, whose bulgy body was pressed to the back of her knees.

"Uh . . . ," she said unsteadily. "Can I help you with anything?"

The man hesitated. She wondered if he was going to speak at all. If he even *could* speak. But then he murmured, "Thank you, miss. I do not believe so."

His voice was soft, low, and polite. The way that he said each word so precisely made his voice seem old-fashioned, too. It sounded out of practice, like an antique that no longer does the job it was made for.

Another wash of cold, followed by a thrill of excitement, raced over Eliza's body.

The strange old clothes. The silent movements. The rusty voice.

She was talking to a ghost.

It took all her willpower to keep from reaching out and grabbing the man's arm, to find out if it was solid or wispy, icy cold or not there at all. Eliza's heart leaped. There was so much evidence to gather! So much material for her research notebook! If this was *the* ghost—the shadow she'd spotted on the street, the source of the sounds in the attic—he must have a reason for haunting this place. She needed to learn more without scaring him away.

"Is this your first time in our shop?" she asked carefully.

The man hesitated again. Eliza caught a twitch of motion on his nearly hidden face, as his eyes traced the path between Eliza and the workroom door.

"It is," he murmured at last.

"But you've been on this street before?" Eliza pushed on. "You've been . . . nearby?"

Behind their plastic sunglasses, the man's eyes homed in on her face. Eliza thought she saw one side of his mouth shift, his lips curving just above the edge of his collar. The ghost was warming up to her! He knew that she understood him! Eliza's heart buzzed in her ribs.

"True," he answered. "I have been nearby."

Eliza wanted to blurt out a hundred questions. Had he lived here? Had he *died* here? What kept him tied to this place? What time was he from? Had anyone but her ever seen him?

While Eliza's brain swirled with things to ask, the man

took another few steps toward the workroom. The dark coat rippled behind him. Eliza followed.

"Oh, that's where my mother's working," she said. "You should probably—"

But the ghost halted long before reaching the door. Again, his body stiffened. He turned his head slowly, until his hidden eyes were aimed straight through the rare plant room, in the direction of the greenhouse. He seemed almost to be sniffing the air, sensing something that Eliza couldn't perceive.

"Is there something that keeps you here?" Eliza whispered.

The ghost didn't answer.

He stood still for so long that Eliza's skin started to itch. Then he turned, very slowly, and gazed straight down at Moggie, who kept herself pressed to Eliza's legs. The dog's curly gray hair stood up in tufts. Her hackles rose. She let out a long, deep growl.

"Moggie," Eliza scolded. "Moggie, *hush.*"

The dog bumped past Eliza, putting herself between the ghost and the back of the shop. She growled again. Louder.

The ghost threw one more look at the workroom door. Then, his shadowy coat sweeping behind him, he wheeled around and strode straight for the front door.

He moved so quickly that Eliza couldn't catch up.

"Wait!" she called, as he shoved through the tinkling door. "Wait! I want to help you!"

But he was already out of her reach.

Eliza charged through the door onto the sidewalk. She looked both ways. She scanned the storefronts across the street.

He had vanished.

Eliza stood for a few seconds, breathing hard. She had lost him.

But for a little while, she had talked to *a ghost*.

And he had talked to her. He had been real.

Eliza's body was so full of joy, it could have let off sparks.

She dashed back into the shop.

The young couple was still there, browsing near the pond.

"Tough customer?" said the man sympathetically.

Eliza smiled. "You could say that."

So they had seen the ghost, too! *More* material for her notebook!

She was mentally preparing her notes when Tommy emerged through the arch of the rare plant room. He stopped at the center of the shop, staring toward the front door. Moggie positioned herself beside him.

"Hey," he whispered to Eliza. "Did something just happen?"

Eliza could have blurted out the whole story. But Tommy's twitchy, anxious movements told her there might be more evidence to collect first. "What do you mean?"

"I just . . . I got the weirdest feeling. Like—like someone was looking right over my shoulder. Breathing in my ear." He shuddered. "But then I looked around, and . . ."

Eliza had to press the excitement out of her voice. "And you were alone?"

Tommy's reply was barely a whisper. "Yeah."

"Hey there, you two!" Mr. Carroll boomed into the shop.

His form filled the entire front door like a tropical-print curtain. "Everything all right while we were gone?"

Eliza beamed back at him. "Everything was great."

Tommy just nodded.

"Glad to hear it!" Mr. Carroll lifted a white bakery box. "There was a cupcake buffet at the reception. The happy couple gave these to us, although if they hadn't, I'd have been tempted to steal them anyway." He gave Eliza a wink. "Come pick your favorites, before I pick them all for myself."

"All right," said Eliza. "Thanks!"

Tommy still didn't speak. He looked down, shaking his hair over his face. In the last clear glimpse she got of them, Eliza thought she noticed something strange in his eyes.

Maybe it was fear.

• • •

After the shop closed for the night, everyone gathered for a gumbo dinner in the Carrolls' apartment. Mr. and Mrs. Carroll and Eliza's mother were all in great spirits, talking about strange plants and stranger customers. Eliza sat in an invisible ray of joy that was all her own.

She had finally met a ghost.

Everything she'd hoped and researched and prepared for was *real*.

It made her want to twirl around the room.

She was dying to tell someone. Someone who would believe her. Who would understand. Maybe she would send a note to Xavier and Chloe later. Or maybe . . .

She glanced across the table at Tommy. While everyone else was in high spirits, Tommy had slumped so far down in his chair that his face barely cleared the tabletop.

"Um . . . Aunt Camila?" he spoke up. "I'm not feeling so well. I think I'll take a walk."

"Oh?" Mrs. Carroll looked concerned. "What's wrong? Did I make the gumbo too spicy? Do you need an antacid?"

"No." Tommy backed quickly away from the table. "Just a little air. I won't go far."

"All right," called his aunt, but Tommy was already out the door.

Eliza jumped up. "Would it be okay if I went with him?"

Under the table, Moggie prodded Eliza's leg with her wet snout.

The Carrolls both smiled, but her mother's face was wary. "I don't know, Eliza. It's getting dark, and you don't know the neighborhood. . . ."

"I'll be with Tommy," Eliza argued. "And we'll stay close to the shop."

"Tell you what," said Mr. Carroll. "Why don't you take Moggie with you? *She* knows the neighborhood. Every tree and hydrant, anyway. And nobody will bother you if you've got this tough old girl along. Am I right?" He aimed this question at Moggie, who answered with a little *Hmmppgh*.

A minute later, Eliza stepped through the front door of Carrolls' Gardens, Moggie's leash in her fist. She just hoped she wasn't too late to catch sight of Tommy. She paused, looking up the sidewalk.

But Moggie didn't pause. The dog took off to the right, dragging Eliza after her.

"Do you smell Tommy? Did he go this way?" Eliza asked.

Moggie pulled harder. Eliza decided to take this as a yes.

Sunset was falling over the neighborhood. A smoky orange sky glowed between the tops of buildings and the fluttering leaves of trees. People filled the sidewalks, strolling into cafés, walking other dogs. Moggie ignored all of them. She lumbered on, snorfling at the pavement, until they reached a corner that Eliza had never turned before.

Moggie yanked to the left.

They sped past a little park that Eliza didn't recognize, and then past a row of sidewalk cafés, Moggie leading the way. Eliza couldn't spot Tommy anywhere. And the night was getting darker, the people all around turning to black and blue shadows. A half-moon floated in the gray sky like a broken cookie in a pond.

"Where is he?" Eliza asked the dog. "Where did Tommy go?"

But at that moment, Moggie had spotted a dog across the street. It was a big shaggy brown mutt, part sheepdog and part mystery, and obviously a stray, with no leash or collar. Moggie gave an enthusiastic *Woof!*

The other dog looked up, startled. It whirled and skittered away.

Moggie took off after it like a furry gray missile.

"Moggie, stop!" Eliza yelled.

The dog didn't seem to hear. She bounded across the street after the mutt, her long pink tongue billowing. Eliza clutched the leash with both hands and hung on for dear life. They whisked through traffic, down busy blocks, around trees, past rows of trash cans, chasing the mutt. At last, Eliza threw herself behind the stone wall of someone's front stoop. Moggie, who couldn't pull a whole staircase along, jerked to a stop. The mutt swerved into an alley and disappeared.

Eliza leaned on the stoop, panting.

The sky had turned from gray to black. Eliza had no idea where they were, except that they were somewhere deep in an unfamiliar city. In her stomach, a cold clump of panic started to form.

"Now what?" she whispered.

Moggie sniffed at Eliza's hand. Then she turned and tugged toward the left. With nothing else to do, Eliza followed.

They turned a corner, and then another. Soon they were passing a familiar Thai café lit by silk lanterns, and a coffee shop with a familiar mural, and just ahead of them loomed the familiar pointed turret of Carrolls' Gardens.

They may not have found Tommy, but at least Moggie had found the way home.

Tired and defeated, Eliza opened the heavy glass door. The bell jingled.

The lights in the store were out. The glow from the street was just strong enough for Eliza to see that she and Moggie had the room to themselves. Moggie, not used to being leashed indoors, wriggled impatiently in her collar. Eliza bent to unclip the leash, and the dog trundled off into the plants.

Eliza made her way toward the stairs. Leaves rustled around her. The sounds from the street grew fainter with each step.

Behind her, in the dimness, there was the click of a door.

At the same moment, Moggie let out a *Woof!*

Eliza whirled around.

A silhouette slumped through the greenery. Eliza recognized its saggy shoulders and messy hair. Tommy.

Relief shot through her, followed by confusion. Because the

only door that could have made that sound was the one to her mother's workroom.

"Tommy!" she called, hurrying closer. "We tried to catch up with you on your walk, but we couldn't find you. You must have just beaten us back here."

"Oh," mumbled Tommy. "I guess so."

It was hard to tell in the dimness, but Tommy seemed to be shaking slightly. A faint sheen of sweat gleamed on his skin.

"Were you in my mom's workroom?" Eliza asked.

Tommy gave her a quick, sharp look. The details of his face were blurred by darkness, but she could still catch the glint of his eyes. "I wanted to check something," he said. "One of the plants your mom and I talked about. I had an idea about its family."

Eliza pictured a set of plants arranged in a cozy circle around a dinner table, but she knew this wasn't the kind of family Tommy meant. She took a step toward him. "Are you feeling okay?"

Tommy stepped back. "What do you mean?"

"At dinner, you said you weren't feeling well. And earlier today, when your aunt and uncle were gone, you said you had a weird, cold feeling. . . ."

Tommy stiffened. "So you followed me?"

"I just wanted to talk to you. Because I think I know what's going on here." She dropped her voice, even though no one but Moggie was there to hear. "Tommy, this place is *haunted*. And today, *I talked to the ghost.*"

Tommy was quiet for so long that Eliza wondered if he hadn't heard her. He took another step backward. "Um . . . ," he said. "Okay."

Eliza's heart plummeted. "You don't believe me?"

"No. I believe you. I just . . ." Tommy shuffled sideways, toward the stairs. "I guess I'm still not feeling so good. I'd better get to bed."

He turned toward the flower department. The lights of a passing car sliced through the shop, coating Tommy's face with just enough light that for an instant Eliza could see every feature in perfect, colorful detail.

That was when she noticed his eyes.

They had been hazel before. She'd caught their color on the rare occasions when he'd made direct eye contact with her: a speckled greenish-brown. It had seemed funny that someone who loved plants would even have plant-colored eyes.

But in that moment, before Tommy turned away, Eliza saw something else.

Tommy's eyes were yellow.

Yellow eyes?? Ghosts?? There sure are some suspicious characters in this chapter! Turn to page 235.

ELIZA FILLED SEVERAL PAGES of her research note-book that night.

She made notes about Tommy's behavior: the nervous way he'd acted after the black-cloaked ghost left the shop, his sneaking into her mother's workroom. And the yellow eyes.

They weren't pale hazel, or light brown, or any other color that belonged in people's eyes. They were *yellow*. An inhuman, solid, burning yellow.

Exactly like the eyes that had stared in at her from the storm-soaked backyard.

But *those* eyes couldn't have been Tommy's. The face around those burning yellow eyes hadn't been Tommy's face. That face had been . . . barely human.

So there was more than one pair of yellow eyes lurking nearby.

That couldn't be a coincidence. Could yellow eyes be

contagious? Or—a breath caught in Eliza's throat—could Tommy be *possessed*?

She pieced through the evidence. The ghost finally manifested itself in the shop. Tommy started feeling strange immediately afterward, and by night, his eyes had changed color.

It all made sense. Possession by spirits wasn't uncommon. Eliza had never encountered it herself, but she'd spent years preparing to. She knew what possession meant: The ghost was using Tommy for something. But what? What did the ghost want?

Eliza scribbled until her hand was sore and her mother insisted that she turn out the lights. Even then, she lay in bed, staring at the ceiling, where she thought she heard the creak of footsteps.

The next morning, Eliza woke up burning with motive and curiosity.

Her mother, who always woke up burning with those things, had gone downstairs ahead of her. But the moment Eliza reached the shop floor, she knew that something had changed.

The door to the workroom hung wide open. Bumping and muttering came from inside. Eliza craned through the doorway.

Instead of bending over the worktable, her mother was crouched in the corner, shoving at a row of potted plants. "No," Eliza heard her mumble. "No. No. No."

"Mom? What's going on?"

"Oh—sweet pea," said her mother distractedly. "A plant is missing."

"Missing?"

"I swear it was on the table when I left the room yesterday, and now it's nowhere."

Eliza glanced around at the greenery. "Which plant?"

"The one with the gold leaves and little red berries."

With a *snuff*, Moggie stepped through the door and moseyed over to rub herself against Eliza's leg. "That little birch-tree-looking thing?" Eliza asked, patting the dog.

"Unfortunately, it's the one I'm still farthest from identifying." Her mother heaved to her feet. She glanced over the specimens nearby. "It may never have been scientifically

identified at all, at least not in this country. If it's lost . . ." Her mother gave a sigh that was almost a growl. "I'll just *kick* myself."

Eliza's mind started to whirl. She hadn't seen any customers go into the workroom. But she had seen someone coming *out*.

Maybe this was what the ghost wanted: It had possessed Tommy in order to make him steal the plant for some reason. But *why*?

"Hey, Mom?" Eliza began. "I—"

A deep voice interrupted her.

"Good morning!" Mr. Carroll called from across the room. "Hope you two slept well! Camila's gumbo always gives me wild dreams. Last night, I was playing basketball against two giant rats, and my teammate was a ficus tree." He sighed. "Those rats wiped the floor with us."

"Last night was fine," Eliza's mother called back distractedly. "It's this morning that's giving me trouble."

"Anything a cup of coffee would fix?" Mr. Carroll offered, heading toward the floral department.

"I'm afraid not. One of the plants is missing. The specimen with the red fruits." Eliza's mother rubbed her forehead. "It was here when I finished work yesterday. . . ."

"It'll turn up!" Mr. Carroll called back. "A customer probably moved it, set it down somewhere it doesn't belong."

"You think a customer came into my workroom?"

Mr. Carroll laughed. "Customers will wander pretty much anywhere. Last year, we found three of them browsing the plants in our living room. I'll put that coffee on, and then I'll help you look."

Eliza's mother gave the workroom a last glance. "Strange," she muttered. "Even the fruit I took from the plant is gone." She headed out the door, Eliza and Moggie trailing behind. "I suppose Winston's right. We'd better search the shop."

"Good morning, everyone!" Mrs. Carroll swept out from the floral department, the fluttering hems of her long skirt swishing behind her. "Good morning," she told a fern. "Good morning, you beauties," she sang to a table of orchids. "And good morning, handsome." She rose onto her tiptoes to kiss Mr. Carroll's cheek. "What's going on down here?"

"We've got a runaway plant," Mr. Carroll answered. "One of the specimens Rachel was working on. I've heard of strawberry runners, but I've never seen a shrub make a break for it before!"

"Oh, Win." Mrs. Carroll twittered. "Next you'll tell us it decided to make like a tree, and *leaf*." She gestured around the sunny room. "I'm sure it's lost in this mess somewhere!"

"Yes," Eliza's mother answered, heading toward one vine-draped corner. "Nothing else is missing. It does seem likely that it was just misplaced."

Eliza hurried after.

Once they were out of the Carrolls' earshot, she whispered, "Mom . . . yesterday evening, after dinner, I saw Tommy coming out of your workroom."

"What?" Her mother thrust her head under a table. Several baby spider plants drummed against her back.

"I saw *Tommy* coming out of your *workroom*," Eliza repeated.

Her mother glanced up through the spider plants. "Did he have the missing plant?"

"No. But he was acting suspicious."

"How so?" Her mother crawled toward the next table. "Did he say anything about what he was doing?"

"He said you two had been talking about some plant's family, and he wanted to take another look."

"That's true," said her mother, from beneath a rack of spiky plants. "We had a great discussion about moonworts."

Eliza, who didn't think the words *great discussion* and *moonworts* belonged in the same sentence, made a skeptical face. "That's not the only suspicious thing." She dropped to her knees beside her mother. "When I asked Tommy what he'd been doing in your workroom, I noticed—"

Just then, Tommy himself shuffled into the shop.

His face was pale. Purplish crescents hung under his downcast eyes. His shoulders were so high and his head was so low that he looked like a shaggy tortoise, one who wished he could disappear straight into himself.

Eliza felt a thump of pity. Poor Tommy. She had to release him from the ghost's hold. And she had to learn what the ghost wanted in order to free the ghost itself.

"I'll tell you later," Eliza whispered to her mother.

She kept a close watch on Tommy for the rest of the morning.

Tommy was slower and even quieter than usual. He sagged through his chores like someone half asleep . . . or like someone under a possessive power. In the late morning, Eliza was huddled just outside the flower department, watching Tommy dust leaves in the rare plant room while Moggie panted into her ear, when suddenly Tommy froze.

He swayed on his feet for a moment. Then, with a stumble, he lurched toward a pot on a high shelf.

Eliza recognized the delicate purple flowers trembling inside. It was monkshood, or wolfsbane, or whatever Tommy had called it. The plant that was poisonous even to touch.

Tommy took down the pot. He seemed to be examining the flowers—maybe even smelling them. Would just inhaling them be enough to make you sick? Eliza was still wondering this when Tommy lifted one hand toward the purple blossoms. Eliza shot to her feet, ready to stop him—but at the last second, Tommy reached up and shoved the plant back onto the shelf. Then he turned, his head bowed even lower, and shuffled out of the room.

That was when Eliza made up her mind.

She found Mr. and Mrs. Carroll in the floral department. Mr. Carroll had just said something that made Mrs. Carroll laugh and smack him on the arm with an overblown tulip. The two of them looked so happy, Eliza hated to spoil it. But Tommy was clearly in danger. She had to tell them why.

Spotting Eliza, Mr. Carroll gave her a quick grin. "Back me up, Eliza," he said, turning toward a high cabinet. "That was an unfair fight. One against *tu*-lip."

"Oh, Win!" giggled Mrs. Carroll.

"Um . . . Mr. and Mrs. Carroll?" Eliza began. Moggie bumped a damp nose against her hand. "I need to talk to you. About Tommy."

"Tommy?" repeated Mrs. Carroll, bending over a floral arrangement. "Is it a hygiene thing? Because I've already talked to him about daily showers."

"No, it's not that." Eliza took a deep breath. "The other

night, when he went for that walk . . . I think maybe he just *said* he was going for a walk and actually never left at all. Because when I got back to the shop, I caught him coming out of my mother's workroom."

Mr. Carroll shuffled supplies in the cabinet. "What was he doing in there?"

"He said he was just looking at something. But today, after that plant disappeared, he was acting even weirder. It's like he's sleepwalking. Or hypnotized." The tendons in Eliza's neck drew tight. "It's like something is affecting him. Something big. Something he's trying to hide."

The Carrolls exchanged a look.

"We'll talk to Tommy," said Mrs. Carroll. "Thank you, dear."

"But—"

Apparently she wasn't being clear. The Carrolls weren't recognizing the danger. "I think something is *forcing* Tommy to act this way," Eliza said intently. "Maybe it forced him to steal the missing plant. And now it's trying to hurt him. According to my observations . . ." She paused for emphasis. "I think Tommy is *possessed.*"

She'd expected some kind of reaction. Disbelief. Confusion. Maybe even insulted anger.

What she hadn't expected was *nothing.*

The Carrolls simply went on with their work. Mr. Carroll kept tidying the cabinets. Mrs. Carroll continued arranging the flowers.

Eliza started to wonder if she'd only imagined saying the words out loud.

At last, Mrs. Carroll gave a gentle nod. "Don't worry," she said. "We're keeping an eye on him, too."

"That's the other thing," said Eliza. "His eyes—"

But she didn't finish.

Mrs. Carroll had just completed her floral arrangement. With a sigh of delight, she placed a final sprig of greenery and then turned to face Eliza. Her smile was as sweet and twinkly as always.

And her eyes . . .

Her eyes were not.

Eliza choked on a breath. She rocked backward, bumping into Moggie's squat, solid form.

Yellow.

Yellow eyes.

"Tommy sure is lucky to have you worrying about him," put in Mr. Carroll, giving Eliza a kindly smile.

Mr. Carroll's eyes had always been deep brown. A warm, gleaming, polished walnut brown.

Not anymore.

Eliza's head spun. Her body felt like ice.

Don't panic, she told herself. *Don't let them* see *you panic, anyway. Now GET OUT OF HERE.*

"Okay." Eliza forced the word out. "Well, if you're keeping an eye on Tommy"—she shuddered. A *yellow* eye!—"then—um—good."

She bolted around the corner and nearly collided with her mother, who was just coming out of the restroom.

"Mom," Eliza whispered desperately, grabbing her mother by the arms. "Meet me up in our room in *five minutes*. It's *important*."

Her mother's left eyebrow rose. "All right," she said. "I was about to take a lunch break anyway."

Eliza tore up the stairs.

In their room, she threw herself down on the bed with her research notebook. She scribbled down everything: Tommy and the monkshood. The Carrolls' reaction to her theory. The color of their eyes. For most of the morning, they'd been distant enough that Eliza hadn't noticed the change. Had the Carrolls' eyes been yellow all day? If she could identify exactly when the change had happened, maybe she could find out where and how they had been possessed. Maybe she could learn where the ghost was *right now*.

From above, there came a soft shushing sound.

Eliza glanced up at the ceiling. She held her breath, keeping perfectly still.

But the stillness was broken by the opening door.

Before her mother could even step inside, Eliza swooped on her like a starving vulture.

"Mom," she said, locking the door and dragging her mother toward the bed. "Can you please sit down? I need to tell you something."

Eliza told the whole story, from the very beginning. She told about the sounds from the attic and the voices in the basement. Mr. Carroll and his secret plant delivery. The black-cloaked ghost. Tommy's secretive behavior. The yellow eyes. She showed her mother her pages of detailed notes. Finally, out of breath, she sagged back on the mattress.

Her mother was quiet for several seconds. She reread Eliza's notes, her gray eyes slicing over the pages.

"This is excellent work," she said at last. "Very thorough."

"So . . . you believe me?"

"I believe that you saw these things," her mother said carefully. "However, I'm not sure you can draw a well-supported scientific conclusion from them. Especially one involving *possession* by *ghosts*."

Hope drained out of Eliza like water through a cracked mug.

Without her mother's help, she was all alone again—alone in a shop full of poisonous plants and yellow-eyed people. How could she explain? How could she connect psychical research and botany in a way that—

Eliza sat up straighter. "Mom, you know how my school took that field trip to Salem last year?"

Her mother's left eyebrow rose. That eyebrow got a lot of exercise when Eliza was around. "Yes?"

"We went to the witch museum," Eliza continued, speaking faster, "and we learned about the witch trials and the hangings and about why the villagers started going crazy and accusing each other of witchcraft in the first place."

"I remember you being disappointed that the museum wasn't creepier."

"Well—yeah. I mean, most people don't believe that the devil actually possessed people in Salem. But there are lots of theories about why it happened. And one of them comes from *botany*." Eliza craned forward. "I guess there's this stuff that grows on corn, and eating it can make you hallucinate—"

"Ergot," said her mother. "And it grows on rye."

"Right," said Eliza. "So they think a bunch of Salem townspeople might have eaten this ergot stuff and started having visions of the devil and black magic."

Her mother nodded slowly. "I've heard the Salem ergot theory. It's an extremely strong one. Ergot poisoning causes shaking, confusion, delusions, even the sensation of being pricked by needles or pins. Exactly what the victims of the supposed *witchcraft* described."

"Well, what if *this*"—Eliza smacked her notebook—"is something like *that*? What if it has to do with the secret plants in the basement and the noises in the attic and the missing plant and the yellow eyes? What if there's some biological, botanical connection between the spirit world and the real world? Like . . ." She paused as the pieces fell into place. "What if a plant could help possess people?"

Her mother took a longer pause. "Like the *Ophiocordyceps*

unilateralis fungus and *Camponotus leonardi* ants," she said softly. Her fingertips began to drum together. "Now, *that* is an interesting line of inquiry."

"Will you help me follow it?" Eliza climbed onto her knees. "Just look at the Carrolls' eyes. That's all. You'll see that they've changed. *Please*, Mom."

Her mother's fingers drummed faster. She stared across the room, and Eliza could practically see the calculations unspooling in her mind.

"I'll get a look if I can," she said.

"And then we need to check the attic," Eliza rushed on. "The Carrolls said there's nothing up there but a mess, remember? But I keep hearing sounds from above. The missing plant might be hidden there. We check the attic, and then the basement, and then anyplace else that a ghost might—"

"Eliza. One step at a time." Her mother took a breath.

"I'll start with the Carrolls' eyes. If you're right about that . . . then we'll pursue your theory."

Eliza launched herself across the bed. "Thank you." She squeezed her mother as tight as she could. "Thank you, Mom."

Her mother squeezed her back. "Don't get too excited yet, sweet pea. Not all theories hold up."

"Oh, I know." Eliza bounced on her knees. "I'm just happy to have the help of another psychical researcher."

Her mother stood up. Looking down at Eliza, she started to smile. "Call me a paranormal botanist."

Eliza grinned back. "Team Stahl," she announced. "Plant Detectives."

Who took that plant with the red berries? What's going on with the creepy yellow eyes? Are there TWO mysteries now? Turn to page 242.

A S HER MOTHER ALWAYS said, in any situation where the outcome is unknown, it's best to minimize the variables. So Eliza stayed upstairs while her mother went back down to the shop. After leaving her phone on the table for Eliza, just in case, her mother headed out the door, and Eliza buckled down for some obsessive thinking and pacing.

Minutes crawled past.

What might have happened by now? Had her mother seen the Carrolls' eyes? Did they notice that she had noticed them? And what about the ghost? Was he nearby, watching, waiting to take possession of someone else?

Eliza's whole body felt tight, like a fishing line snagged on something huge and deep, something that refused to break the surface. Even stretching didn't help. After ten sets of toe touches and twenty head rolls, Eliza decided to up the ante and take a hot shower.

She stepped out of the old-fashioned bathroom fifteen minutes later, feeling lightly cooked and a lot more pliable. She headed toward the bed to study her notes.

But her research notebook wasn't there.

Eliza glanced around. Her pen was lying beside the bed, just where she'd left it. But no notebook.

Eliza looked under the bed. She looked under her mother's bed. She checked her box and her backpack. Then she looked everywhere else: The bathroom. The mini fridge. Under the cushions of the window seat.

Nothing.

Her heart thudded. All the searching was pointless; she'd left the notebook on the bed, she was certain. Her mom wouldn't have taken it without even mentioning it. This could mean only one thing: Someone else had come into their room. Someone had crept to Eliza's bed while she was shut behind the bathroom door, and had taken away her notebook and the precious data in it.

Eliza flew to the door and opened it just enough to peer through.

The hallway outside was quiet.

But at the far end, where the next flight of stairs dwindled downward, Eliza thought she caught the disappearing edge of a shadow.

She couldn't see it clearly, but the way it moved—low and hunched, like an animal—made her pretty sure it wasn't Tommy's. Muggie must have followed her up the stairs.

Moggie wouldn't have stolen her notebook, would she? Not unless there was bacon pressed between the pages. And there wasn't.

Eliza held her breath.

But the shadow was already gone, if it had ever been there at all.

. . .

In late afternoon, her mother burst through the doorway. She locked the door, marched straight to the table, and set down a brown paper package.

"You were right," she said matter-of-factly as Eliza ran to meet her. "Yellow eyes. *Yellow* eyes." She stared into the distance for a moment. Then, shaking herself, she reached for Eliza's arm. "Sweet pea, you feel like chicken someone just pulled out of the freezer. Do you need a sweater?"

Eliza didn't even hear the question. "*Now* do you believe me?"

"I believe, as you do, that something strange is going on here." Her mother's voice was brisk but low. "It seems likely that this strangeness has to do with the missing plant— and considering that the Carrolls both live and work here, it seems likely that the root of this mystery is somewhere on the premises."

"What's in the package?"

"Keys." Her mother dumped the packet onto the table. A half-dozen skeleton keys clunked out. "From the antiques store next door. There are only so many different types of old locks."

Hope started to beat in Eliza's chest. "You mean . . ."

"First we have some dinner," her mother cut her off. The tiniest curve of a smile began to form on her lips. "We wait until the Carrolls are likely to be asleep. And *then* we go to the attic and try these keys out."

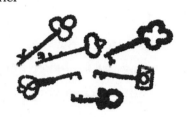

Eliza smiled back.

• • •

Just after ten o'clock, the lights in the Carrolls' apartment blinked off. Eliza, who had been watching them from the turret's window seat, gave her mother a nod. They gathered their tools and slipped out into the hallway. Eliza wore her backpack of ghost-hunting equipment. Her mother carried a hefty flashlight. Its beam led them down the hall, straight to the keyhole of the attic door.

The first three skeleton keys didn't fit. Eliza's shoulders were growing painfully tight when her mother slid key number four into the lock. There was a *click*.

The attic door swung open.

The Stahls tiptoed through. Her mother led the way up a set of narrow, dingy stairs. At the top, they paused, listening to the quiet. Her mother reached up and tugged the chain of a hanging light. Its dirty bulb sputtered on.

Mrs. Carroll was right: The attic was a mess. A sloping, fly-specked, cobweb-draped mess. Broken vases and planters littered the corners. The floor was strewn with half-empty sacks and crumpled paper. Rickety shelves lined the walls, stacked with bottles and jars and jugs whose labels were almost too faded to read.

"Well," murmured her mother. "There's no one here now."

"Nope," Eliza murmured back. "But somebody *was* here."

She pointed to a wooden crate in the center of the room. Its edges were covered with a thick fur of dust, but the middle had been swept clean.

Her mother bent down for a closer look. "You're right. Someone used this surface. And quite recently." She dropped to her knees, sweeping the beam of her flashlight across the floor.

Meanwhile, Eliza checked the nearest corner. Through a window, she could see the pointed metal roof of the turret, just outside. There were no cold spots, as far as she and her thermometer could tell; if anything, the attic was too warm, stuffy with the trapped heat of long summer days. Eliza took out the candle and lit it. Its flame burned a steady gold. The Spectral Translator didn't move. Still, Eliza could sense that something had happened here. Something secret. She could feel it wavering in the air, like a fading scent.

Her mother gave a sharp gasp.

"What?" Eliza hurried closer. "What is it?"

"A leaf." Her mother lifted something from the floorboards. "It's from the missing plant."

Eliza looked at the leaf on her mother's palm. It was limp and gold, with a vague diamond shape. "Are you sure?"

"Absolutely. The distinctive color. The rhombic shape." Her mother frowned. "But how did it get *here*? That's the question."

"Maybe the rest of the plant is here, too," Eliza whispered.

They searched every shelf, every dented box, every burlap sack. They found nothing but a lot of ancient garden supplies and many extremely long-dead beetles.

"No other sign of it," sighed her mother at last. "The plant *was* here, or someone who handled it was here. And now it's gone."

Eliza's shoulders sagged. "Why would somebody—"

She was halfway through the question when from nearby there came a soft, metallic *click*.

Eliza and her mother froze.

For an instant, Eliza wondered if the click had been the cocking of a gun. An instant later, she realized the truth. What they'd heard was the sound of a locking door.

The attic! Finally!! I KNEW that place was important! Turn to page 244.

ELIZA'S MOTHER HURRIED DOWN the steps, the beam of her flashlight bouncing on the scuffed planks. She tugged at the doorknob. "It won't even budge."

"Can you use the key?" Eliza asked.

Her mother aimed the flashlight at the knob. "There's no keyhole on the inside." She slammed her shoulder against the door's solid surface. "I don't believe I can break this down."

"The Carrolls locked us in," Eliza breathed.

Her mother climbed a few steps before replying. "That does seem like a safe conclusion. There's no one else in the building, as far as we know. And there's no way it was accidental. Anyone at the door would have seen the attic light burning. And they would have needed a key."

"They know we're onto them," Eliza whispered as her mother reached the top of the flight. "They had to get rid of us before we could tell anyone else about the weird plant and the yellow eyes. The ghost who's possessing them must have made them do it."

Her mother folded her arms. "There's one problem with that theory," she said. "They *haven't* gotten rid of us." She flashed Eliza a quick, dry smile. "Let's weigh our options. First, we could call the police."

"Call them how?"

"With my phone." Her mother held out a hand. "I left it with you earlier."

Eliza felt something crumble in the base of her stomach. "I left it downstairs. I didn't think of it when . . . Mom, I'm sorry."

"Don't be," said her mother briskly. "It's my phone. My fault. All right. Other options." She scanned the room, aiming her flashlight at one of the windows at the attic's far ends. "Climbing out a window isn't much use when we're on the fourth floor. Yelling for help does nothing if only the Carrolls can hear us." She frowned. "No phone. No help. No one else who knows where we are."

Eliza sidled closer. "What do you think they're going to do to us?"

Her mother was quiet for a moment, considering. "At this point, I could only make a wild guess, but I don't care to collect enough evidence to make a decent one. We can't just wait around on the chance that someone will let us out. We need something that can take down a door."

"Like a screwdriver or a crowbar?"

"Something like that." Her mother's eyes took on the faraway look they usually only got in laboratories and libraries. "Eliza, may I borrow your candle?"

Eliza passed it over. Her mother hurried off toward a set of rickety shelves.

Without her candle, Eliza burrowed through the boxes again, no longer worried about keeping quiet. She found nothing that would help them to escape.

"No luck," she sighed, turning around.

"Down here," called a voice from the bottom of the stairs.

Her mother was crouched by the attic door, wedging a scrap of fabric around the doorframe. Several jars and bottles of old chemicals—fertilizer or pesticides or Eliza couldn't guess what—were scattered around her feet. Halfway up the steps, a battered fire extinguisher sat beside the burning candle.

"What are you doing?" Eliza asked.

"Something *extremely* irresponsible." Her mother flashed Eliza a sharp look. "These are *not* ideal conditions. I want you to know that," she continued, pouring the contents of one bottle onto the fabric around the door. "But I'm not going to let anyone trap my daughter in an attic indefinitely. It's like something out of one of your ghost stories."

"Huh." Eliza started to smile. "You're right!"

Her mother tucked the fire extinguisher under one arm. She stuffed a wad of newspaper into the neck of an empty plastic bottle, its end sticking out like a tissue in a dispenser. Then she picked up the candle.

"Stand back," she told Eliza. "Stand *way* back."

Eliza rushed to the far wall.

Her mother lit the newspaper and blew out the candle in one quick motion. Then, running up the steps, she threw the burning bottle over her shoulder toward the attic door.

The explosion wasn't like the ones Eliza had heard in movies: deep and rumbling, complete with slow-motion images of rolling fireballs. This was one quick, whooshing *BANG* that seemed to suck all the air out of the room. A wave of heat swept over her face.

She and her mother skidded back toward the top of the steps. Sour, chemical-scented smoke poured up the staircase. Fire crackled in the doorway and along the edges of the dingy attic stairs. The door gaped on one intact hinge.

"Let's hope this is still functional." Her mother passed Eliza the candle and aimed the fire extinguisher. A gout of white foam spattered through the stairwell. The flames hissed out. "That was fortunate." Her mother dropped the extinguisher. It hit the attic floor with a clunk. "As I said, those were *not* ideal conditions. Far too many variables. Too many risks." She grabbed Eliza's hand. "Hold your breath. Come on."

Together, they charged down the steps, leaped over the soot and foam, and flew out through the open doorway.

"Hey, Mom?" said Eliza, as they ran back toward their room. "You would make a really great ghost hunter."

Her mother threw her a half-smile. "And I've always thought you'd make an excellent scientist."

They raced through the door.

"Grab your most important things," her mother instructed. "We'll worry about the rest later. Ten seconds and we're out of here."

Eleven seconds later, with Eliza's tablet and Poe collection in her backpack and her mother's laptop bag swinging over her shoulder, they barreled back into the hall.

They raced down the stairs, past the entrance to the Carrolls' apartment. Eliza heard voices and movement from inside. She and her mother ran faster, plunging down the steps into the darkness of the shop. Behind them, the voices grew louder. A door banged. Footsteps pounded away up the third-floor stairs.

The Stahls rushed through the leafy shadows.

"I'm going to grab my notes from the workroom," hissed her mother. "If that missing plant is at the root of this—excuse the pun—we can't lose all proof that it ever existed."

The workroom was darker still. Her mother flicked on the flashlight and made a beeline for the table. "I was afraid of this," she muttered.

"What?"

"They're gone. My notes. My sketches. Everything involving that plant." She whirled back to Eliza. "Someone is trying to hide every bit of evidence that you and I have collected. We're clearly not safe here, either. Let's go."

Grabbing Eliza by the arm, her mother charged out of the workroom.

They were still several steps from the front door when the shop lights flashed on.

Eliza and her mother spun around, blinking, blinded.

"Rachel!" screamed a voice.

Mrs. Carroll came flying toward them, her pink silk robe fluttering. Mr. Carroll jogged behind her. After them rushed Tommy and Moggie.

Her mother shoved Eliza behind her back. She grabbed the largest, spikiest cactus within reach, holding it in front of her like a spear. "Stay back!" she commanded.

But the Carrolls didn't pause. They rushed closer, leaves waving wildly in their wake, until Eliza could see their faces clearly. All of them had bright yellow eyes. And all of them, except for Moggie, wore nearly identical looks of fear.

"Rachel! Eliza!" Mrs. Carroll gasped. "*Please* say you two are all right!"

Her mother tightened her grip on the cactus. *"All right?"* she repeated. Her hedge-trimmer voice was sharper than ever. "You trap us in your attic and then you ask if we're *all right?*"

"Trap you?" Mrs. Carroll's yellow eyes widened. "Is that what happened?"

"Somebody else must have gotten in here," panted Mr. Carroll. He pressed a hand to his chest. "When that bang from above woke us, I think my heart stopped."

Her mother's eyes slashed between the Carrolls. "You're saying that none of you locked us in?"

"Absolutely not!" Mrs. Carroll clasped her hands. "When we heard that explosion, and we woke up and realized our apartment had been broken into, and we rushed upstairs to find your room empty and the attic door destroyed, we could only imagine—" She broke off with a sob.

Her mother lowered the cactus very slightly. "How do you know someone broke into your apartment?"

Mrs. Carroll twisted her hands tighter. "Because the plant—the one with the red berries—*it's been stolen!*"

For a second, Eliza and her mother stared at the Carrolls.

Mr. Carroll, who apparently slept in a Carrolls' Gardens T-shirt and shiny basketball shorts, wrapped an arm around Mrs. Carroll's heaving shoulders. Tommy wavered behind them both, gazing at Eliza through a messy hank of hair.

"But that plant was *already* stolen," said Eliza at last, feeling like she might as well have said *Water is wet* or *Moggie's breath smells* since she was just stating the obvious.

"Oh, Eliza. Oh, Rachel." Mrs. Carroll's voice dripped

with tears. "We are so sorry. When that plant disappeared before . . . *we* were the ones who stole it." She spread her shaking hands. "Now it's been stolen by *someone else*."

"It's the truth," Tommy spoke up. He looked straight into, Eliza's eyes. "And—um—with what that plant can do, now we're all in *real* trouble."

Whoa, that was unexpected! Turn to page 248.

EVERYONE STOOD PERFECTLY STILL for a moment. The pond bubbled softly in its corner. Green fronds nodded around them.

"We shouldn't stay here," murmured Tommy. "Too many windows."

Eliza glanced around. The darkness outside and the light from within turned the windowpanes to mirrors. All she could see was a bunch of tense, pajama-clad people in a forest of plants. Anyone—any*thing*—could have been staring straight in.

"Let's move into the workroom," Mrs. Carroll suggested weakly. "Then we'll explain everything."

Eliza looked up at her mother.

Mrs. Stahl gave everyone else the kind of look that could have peeled the bark off a pine tree. "All right," she said, slowly setting down the cactus. "But I've got the police on speed dial."

Inside the workroom, Mrs. Carroll sagged against the table, looking like a flower beaten to the ground by hard rain. Tommy and Mr. Carroll and Moggie stood protectively beside her. Eliza and her mother stayed side by side, close to the door.

"Well, I guess we should begin at the beginning," said Mr. Carroll, in a voice that boomed a lot less than usual. "As I've said, we bring in plants from all over the world. Most of our growers and dealers are one-hundred-percent aboveboard. But a few of them are a little . . . *under*board."

"A very few," added Mrs. Carroll limply.

"We've worked with one dealer for years. He's a part-time fisherman, part-time explorer, part-time treasure hunter. He brings us samples from his travels. Things nobody else has." Mr. Carroll's voice got even softer. "Because nobody is supposed to have them."

Her mother sucked in a breath. "I see."

Eliza glanced back and forth between Mr. Carroll's guilty face and her mother's hard one. "What do you see?"

"He's a poacher," said her mother sharply. She looked down at Eliza. "There are strict regulations regarding imported plants. Foreign species can become invasive. They can carry pests or diseases. They can be endangered or protected in their own lands. And the Carrolls, apparently, have been working with this poacher to smuggle rare plants into this country and to sell them on."

"It's true." Mr. Carroll, in his huge T-shirt and shiny

shorts, looked like a half-deflated parade balloon. "Leif makes his deliveries in secret, to the basement door. We pay him under the table. He disappears again."

"So *that's* what you were doing in the basement the other night," Eliza blurted.

Mr. Carroll's yellow eyes flicked to her. There was no surprise in them, only guilt and exhaustion. "That's right."

"We truly didn't think this was so wrong," said Mrs. Carroll. "The plants Leif brings us are carefully contained and monitored. Many of them we sell to laboratories, places that will use them for *good*. . . ."

"The missing plant was one of Leif's deliveries, I assume?" said Eliza's mother. "What else do you know about it? Why would someone steal that plant and no others?"

The Carrolls traded a look.

"I'm going to let Tommy answer that one," said Mr. Carroll. "I'd better go check the rest of the building."

"By yourself, Win?" said Mrs. Carroll worriedly.

"It's all right." He gave her a small smile. "If anyone's still here . . . I'll sniff them out."

With one more look at his family, Mr. Carroll and his shiny basketball shorts swished through the door.

"So. Um." Tommy cleared his throat. Eliza had seen Tommy look uncomfortable plenty of times, but now he looked like if he could have folded himself into a ball tiny enough to disappear into his own belly button, he would have. "I . . . um . . . I like botany. Not that I'm a botanist or anything. But when Uncle Win and Aunt Camila get new things in the shop, sometimes I try to study them. I had a little space set up in the attic, where I could concentrate and do experiments and stuff. In private."

"So it was *you* making noise in the attic!" Eliza burst out. "How come nobody told us?"

"Nobody knew. I didn't *want* anybody to know." Tommy's face was flushed. "Because—I just—I wanted to keep it to myself. At least until I knew what I was doing."

Eliza couldn't help nodding at this. She understood how Tommy felt. If you knew 99 percent of people wouldn't understand your interests anyway, it was easier to keep them to yourself.

"Anyway," Tommy resumed, "I'd taken some samples from that plant with the red fruits. A couple of leaves. Some berries. Then one night, when I was working in the attic, half of one of the berries rolled off my table onto the floor. And before I could pick it up . . . Moggie ate it."

Everyone's eyes flashed to the dog. Moggie panted happily at all of them.

"I was so scared that she would get sick. And it would be all my fault." Tommy rubbed the dog's ear. "So I watched her really closely. I took notes on everything she did. What she ate. When she

134

drank. When she . . . used the fire hydrant. And she was totally fine. Totally normal. So . . ." He took a breath. "After I did the skin test, and the lip test . . . I ate one of the berries myself."

Eliza's mother's eyes narrowed. "And what were the effects?"

"At first, nothing. It tasted fine. I felt fine. But then . . ." Tommy's voice got even mumblier. "Um . . . well, I found out why the berry didn't do anything to Moggie." He said the next words directly to the floor. "I woke up in the middle of the night, and. . . . um . . . I was a dog."

It was so quiet in the workroom that Eliza could hear each of Moggie's panting breaths.

"What?" Eliza asked at last, because no one else did.

"My bed's by a window." Tommy rubbed his own shaggy head. "Later, with a little experimenting, I figured out that it was because of the moonlight. Moonlight, plus the berry, made me a dog."

Everyone was quiet again.

"Tommy," said Eliza's mother as kindly as she could, "do you think that perhaps you were dreaming? Maybe you watched a werewolf movie and then you had some of your aunt's dream-inducing gumbo, and—"

"No." Tommy shook his head. His voice grew clearer. "It wasn't a dream. And there's proof. I changed back when I got out of the moonlight, but *my eyes didn't.*"

"I suppose it's possible that the berry changed your pig-mentation," said her mother, still very kindly, "but as for the rest, it's far more likely that it induced some sort of hal-lucination. I'm sure it felt real, but what you're describing is scientifically—"

"It's scientifically impossible," Tommy interrupted. "I know. But it happened. I tested it again the next night, once the moon came out. It was exactly the same." He rushed on before anyone could argue. "After I knew what the plant did, I moved it up to the attic, just to keep it safe until I figured out what to do. But then you all were searching the whole place for it, so I knew I had to move it again, and Aunt Camila and Uncle Win kept asking me what was wrong, so finally, I just brought the plant down to the apartment and told them." Tommy shared a glance with his aunt. "They didn't believe me, either. Not until they tried it for themselves."

Eliza's mother turned to Mrs. Carroll. "You ate the fruit?"

Mrs. Carroll's hands fussed with the silk belt of her robe. "I know it sounds impossible," she began, "but there's so much we have yet to discover about the natural world. Isn't that what you said, Eliza? That the supernatural is just the natural that's waiting to be understood?"

Eliza held very still. It *did* sound impossible. But she believed in ghosts with total certainty. Was it so impossible that werewolves—or weredogs—existed, too? Couldn't the ghost, the plant, and this impossible effect all be tied together somehow? Didn't they pretty much *have* to be?

"Mom." She nudged her mother's arm. "Don't you think it might be true?"

Her mother gave a laugh with all the air squashed out of it. "Do I think this story *might* be true? Perhaps, in all the alternate universes and infinite timelines that theoretically exist, there is one where eating a berry turns a person into a dog. But I don't believe that we are in it."

Tommy exhaled hard. "Fine. We'll prove it. There's enough moonlight. Come on, Aunt Camila."

Tommy and Mrs. Carroll—who looked extremely reluctant—headed out the workroom door. Moggie stayed beside Eliza.

"I'm not sure what we're waiting for," said Eliza's mother after a moment. "Because we are not *actually* waiting for our hosts to turn into dogs."

Eliza didn't answer. A funny, tickling feeling ran up the backs of her arms. Was it a spectral presence? Mere anticipation? Before she could be sure, Moggie jumped up with a loud *Woof!* She barreled out the workroom door, with Eliza and her mother tagging after.

The shop lights had been turned out again. The Stahls followed Moggie through the darkness, around a rack of orchids, past the cacti, toward the silvery splotch of moonlight that fell through the front windows.

There, on the moonlit floor, one draped in baggy pajama pants and the other swamped in a pink silk robe, were two golden-eyed dogs. The dog in the robe was a Boston terrier, petite and bright faced. The dog in the pajama pants was the shaggy brown mutt Eliza and Moggie had chased through the streets the night before.

Eliza gasped.

Moggie bounded toward the dogs, snuffling their faces and bumping them off their paws.

"All right, Tommy and Camila." Eliza's mother folded

her arms. "I don't know where you're hiding, or why you've decided to play this prank," she said loudly and sternly. "I would guess it's to cover up your own illegal activities involving the smuggled and now *missing* plant, but whatever the reason, I—"

"Oh, it's not a prank, Rachel," said the Boston terrier. Mrs. Carroll's voice sounded almost natural coming out of the dog's little mouth. "As I said, I know it seems impossible. But it's real."

"Science and magic," mumbled the brown mutt.

Eliza's mother let out a sound that Eliza had never heard her make before. "But ... molecular ..." She sputtered. "Can't ... physiological ... *berries* ..."

Eliza took a steadying grip on her mother's arm. "Look at the evidence, Mom," she whispered. "Just look."

At that moment, a bulldog in shiny basketball shorts came trundling through the room.

"Well, looks like our secret's out, huh?" it boomed in Mr. Carroll's voice. "Hello, Eliza and Rachel. I was checking the greenhouse, accidentally hit a beam of moonlight, and *bang*—dog town." The bulldog chuckled. "No sign or smell of any intruders, though. Whoever was here is gone."

Eliza's mother made a choking sound.

Eliza patted her mom on the back, hoping her smile wasn't too smug. The natural and the supernatural were coming together right in front of their eyes!

"Well ...," her mother choked out at last. "I suppose

my reaction doesn't matter. These are the conditions. We'll simply have to function within them." She swayed dizzily. "The most important question here is: If it's not with you, then who has that plant right now?"

"The ghost," said Eliza immediately. Honestly, didn't everyone know this already?

"Eliza, there is no *ghost*." Her mother looked down at her. "The Carrolls are not possessed. They are berry-eating weredogs. . . ." She stopped to rub her face with one shaky hand. "But they are not possessed."

"But what about the ghost—or whatever it was—that I talked to in the shop? The one in the black cloak who's been lurking around?" Eliza demanded. "What about the yellow eyes I saw in the backyard? What about my stolen research notebook and your stolen notes? The Carrolls didn't take them, right?" All the dogs—except Moggie, who was sniffing Mr. Carroll's backside—shook their heads. "What else could it be?"

"The most likely, most *rational* explanation is that the thief is just another person who knows about the plant's powers." Her mother turned to the Carrolls. "Besides the six of us, who knows that the plant was here?"

Mr. Carroll shook his jowly head. "Just Leif."

"Let's start there. Mr. Carroll, would you go and fetch him, please?" Eliza's mother froze, realizing what she'd just said. Her eyes widened. "I mean . . ."

But Mr. Carroll had broken out with a jolly guffaw. "Fetch him!" he chucked, trotting toward the back of the shop. "That's a good one! Maybe I'll get you a newspaper and some slippers, too!"

WHAT ... JUST ... HAPPENED? Turn to page 252.

16

AFTER HIDING FOR A while in the floral department, away from all beams of moonlight, Mr. Carroll emerged looking like his usual self. He made a dash for the back door.

"I'm going to move fast and stick to the shadows!" he shouted over his shoulder. "I don't think my paws could reach the brake!"

The others headed down to the basement, where there was no danger of moonlight reaching them. Eliza and her mother gave the Carrolls some privacy—Mrs. Carroll had explained that the issue of clothing could be tricky, because you didn't always manage to keep on what you were wearing before and after the change—by waiting behind a row of shelves.

"I still can't believe this," her mother muttered to Eliza. "It's all utterly . . . *wrong*."

"I know what you mean," said Eliza thoughtfully. "I

would have guessed Mrs. Carroll would be a poodle, not a terrier."

Her mother's left eyebrow rose.

"Here we are!" sang Mrs. Carroll, fluttering around the shelves in her usual two-legged form. "Thank you for your patience."

Tommy shuffled after her, his cheeks red, his eyes on the floor. Eliza noticed that he'd put his T-shirt on backward.

"You know," Eliza said quietly, as her mother and Mrs. Carroll began discussing the basement's security, "I can't believe I didn't recognize you on our walk the other night."

Tommy looked at her shoes.

"Really," Eliza pushed on. "I mean, even as a dog, you still look like *you*."

Tommy snorted.

"I don't mean that as an insult. I think magically transforming into another creature is really cool."

Now Tommy looked at her chin. "It's not that cool," he mumbled. "I mean—yeah, it's amazing. To change. To see the world as another animal. And the sense of smell is like a *superpower*." He hesitated. "But it's freaky, not being able to control it. Knowing any time a beam of moonlight hits me, I'm not really *me* anymore. Plus, I'm sure there are zillions of scientists like your mom who'd love to run tests on us, take tissue samples, keep us in big glass tanks and stare at us. . . ." He shuddered.

"My mom wouldn't do that," said Eliza. "Probably."

143

Tommy rubbed his arms. "And now I'm stuck keeping this huge secret for the rest of my life. How am I supposed to do anything normal? Like go to college? Or just leave the house after dark? I don't want to live like that forever. I even thought, if I made myself sick enough, maybe I could get the berry out of my system. . . ."

"Is that why you took down the monkshood?"

Tommy met her eyes for a split second. "It's stupid, but I thought . . . *wolfsbane*. It might work. But I knew it was too dangerous. I couldn't go through with it."

"So, how does it feel?" Eliza overheard her mother asking Mrs. Carroll. She and Tommy moved closer. "The transformation itself, that is?"

"Mostly it feels itchy. All that hair sprouting everywhere." Mrs. Carroll gave a delicate shiver. "And it's uncomfortable. It's like being squeezed into an outfit that's much, *much* too small for you. I'm always quite sore afterward."

"I know some stretches that might help," Eliza offered.

But she didn't get to demonstrate. Before anyone could speak again, the basement door banged open. Mr. Carroll hustled down the steps toward them, his meaty hand clamped around the arm of another man—a man with a battered sweater and tangled hair under a knit cap.

"Leif," said Mrs. Carroll sweetly. "How are you, dear?"

Leif glanced around the basement. His skin was weather-beaten and sunburned, almost the color of a sliced grapefruit. His eyes were sharp and bright and definitely *not* yellow, Eliza noticed. They were more of a mirror-y blue—a shade that took in everything and reflected it straight back out again.

"All right. Thanks," he said shortly. "You?"

Eliza recognized that voice. It was the raspy one she'd heard speaking to Mr. Carroll before. And it was nothing like the soft, polite, old-fashioned voice of the black-cloaked ghost.

"So, Leif," boomed Mr. Carroll, "we've got some questions. Have a seat."

"More comfortable on my feet," said Leif. He took another twitchy look around. "Don't like these enclosed spaces. Too still for my taste."

"Have a seat." Mr. Carroll's jolly tone didn't change, but his big hand grabbed Leif by the shoulder and shoved him down onto a waiting crate. "We need to know more about one of the plants you brought us."

"I'm a supplier, not a gardener," said Leif with a shrug and a nervous grin. "I don't know poison oak from the Oakland A's."

"We need to know where a specific plant came from," said Mr. Carroll, as though Leif hadn't spoken.

The explorer gave a short, dry laugh. It sounded like two pieces of toast scratching together. "You want me to remember one little plant? You might as well ask me to remember one time I tied my shoes."

Eliza's mother thrust out her cell phone. On its screen was a photo of the red-berried plant. "It's this one."

The change in Leif was instantaneous. His twitchy body stilled. His face went flat.

"Thought it might be that one," he murmured.

"Where did you find it?" her mother asked.

Leif kept silent for several seconds. His hands, covered with tattoos of blue-inked constellations, clenched and unclenched anxiously. "On our last trip, we went up the Atlantic coast," he said at last. "Maine. Nova Scotia. Chains of little islands. Collected ferns and wildflowers, mostly. Checked out the site of an old shipwreck, found a couple decent pieces. But then one night . . ." His words slowed. "Out of nowhere, there came this little island. It wasn't on any of the maps. We found a cove. Went ashore."

He paused, the Big Dipper rippling below his knuckles. "I've visited a thousand islands. But there was something off about this one. Everywhere we went, we felt like we were being watched. Or *hunted*." He swallowed. "We never saw what was watching us, but we heard rustles in the underbrush, really soft and slow. Could have been a bear, I suppose, or a mountain lion, or . . . something else. Whatever it was, it was stalking us." Leif nodded at the picture. "Quick as I could, I dug up this plant. And we got the heck out of there.

"But that feeling, that we were being stalked . . . it came with us." He clasped his shaking hands together. "Now it was on the boat. We still couldn't see it, but we noticed things. Sounds. Objects that moved. Shadows that definitely weren't . . . *human*. It didn't leave until we docked and finally got that plant off board."

He glanced around at everyone, looking like he wished he could laugh at himself. But Eliza saw the fear in his pale eyes. "I know this sounds like drunken sailor talk. But I swear it's true. Believe it if you like."

"I believe you," said Eliza.

Eliza's mother tapped her fingertips together. "Say your conclusions are accurate. That someone or something was watching you—or perhaps watching the plant. Wouldn't it be safe to assume that whoever it was is also aware of the plant's properties? And that whoever it was may be the thief we are looking for now?"

"It was the ghost!" Eliza exclaimed. "It all makes sense!"

"Hang on," said Leif. "What properties are we talking about?"

Eliza's mother took a deep breath and closed her eyes. "It appears that ingestion of the plant's fruit transforms a human into a canine."

Mr. Carroll let out a sudden belly laugh. "You know, we should call the plant a *dogwood tree*! Too bad the name's already taken!"

147

"Oh, Win!" laughed Mrs. Carroll.

"Mr. Carroll, *please*," said Eliza's mother. "Now, we should try to determine what our thief plans to do with the plant. He might want it for himself. Or he might plan to profit from it somehow. Who would pay most for this sort of ability?"

"Dog lovers?" offered Mrs. Carroll.

"Movie people," suggested Mr. Carroll. "It would be a lot easier to train Lassie if Lassie was really a person."

Eliza's mother frowned. "Genetic researchers would be fascinated. It would also be extremely interesting to the military, and to the intelligence community. Spies would make great use of it. So would organized and unorganized crime . . ."

Leif stared up at Eliza's mother, looking dazed. "Run this by me one more time," he said. "You're saying that plant turns people into dogs?"

"Care for a demonstration?" asked Mr. Carroll. "Head upstairs and find a moonbeam with me, and—"

"There's no time," said Eliza's mother. "We need to act swiftly. The thief may already have gotten away."

Eliza raised her hand. "I think we should—"

"We can search the neighborhood," suggested Mr.

Carroll. "Camila and Tommy and I, in dog form. We'll follow our noses right to the culprit!"

Eliza raised her hand again. "Ghost-hunting techniques might—"

"That's a decent start," her mother said over her. "In the meantime, if I enlarge the photo of the plant on my laptop and set it somewhere in view of the windows, it might be mistaken for another sample of the real thing and lure the thief back in."

"Can't hurt to try," said Mr. Carroll.

"But it's clear that supernatural powers are—" Eliza began.

"Or we could just put out some kibble!" blurted Leif. He gave a nervous laugh, then bit his lips. "Sorry. I'm out of my depth here."

"We all are," said Eliza's mother briskly. "But we'll just have to plunge in. All right, everyone. Let's move."

Everybody but Eliza and Moggie rushed up the stairs.

Eliza started to follow, and then looked down at Moggie, who panted hopefully up at her.

"I was *going* to say," Eliza told the dog, "considering that this mystery combines natural and supernatural elements, we should try ghost-summoning techniques." She sighed and crouched down to scratch Moggie's ears. "They can believe in a plant that turns people into dogs, but they still don't believe *me*."

She and Moggie padded up into the shop. The Carrolls had already vanished. Eliza could hear her mother and Leif in the distance, murmuring about which windows had the best views.

"To summon a ghost," Eliza told Moggie, "it helps to know the ghost's name. But we don't. The next best thing is to use an item that once belonged to that ghost, something important to . . ."

But now even Moggie was ignoring her. The dog put her snout to the floor and turned away, snuffling loudly.

"What?" Eliza asked. "Is this the way the ghost went?"

Moggie snuffled across the rare plant room and toward the floral department. She sniffed straight up to the base of the stairs. Instead of climbing them, she lumbered to the right, toward a big tub full of mums. Then she bent her front legs, put her rump in the air, and shoved her head as far behind the tub as it would go. Sounds of loud snorting filtered out through the flowers.

"What is it?" Eliza knelt beside the dog. "Did you lose a dog treat down there?" She shoved the tub aside.

Behind it, wedged against the wall, was one bright jewel-red berry.

Eliza grabbed it.

She recognized it: size, shape, and color. The berry must have fallen from the missing plant, maybe when the ghost had smuggled it away.

"Good girl, Moggie," she whispered.

Eliza slipped the berry into her pocket.

If no one else took her ghost hunting seriously, then she would hunt this ghost on her own.

And now she had a plan.

What's up with this Leif guy?
I bet he knows more than he's letting on ...
Turn to page 253.

17

ELIZA STOOD ALONE IN the dark greenhouse.

Shut outside the glass doors, Moggie harrumphed, licked the panes, and finally moseyed away. Eliza felt sorry for excluding her, but she needed to focus. Now the room was so quiet, she could almost hear the hundreds of plants breathing, leaves unfurling bit by bit.

By touch, she dug through her backpack and pulled out the candle and matches. She lit the wick, and the greenhouse filled with a faint gold glow. The glass-paned walls reflected a hundred copies of Eliza's dimly lit face. She looked a little scared. And determined. And excited.

Sometimes she and Xavier and Chloe had practically seen Bloody Mary surfacing in their toothpaste-flecked bathroom mirrors. She knew what to do next. So what if she didn't know the ghost's name? She had something important to him tucked right in her pocket.

Setting the candle on a table, Eliza pulled out the berry.

She cupped it in her palm, her fingers open just enough that its redness glinted in the candlelight.

"I call you," she whispered.

It felt funny to be talking to no one, not even a dog. Eliza swallowed and spoke again. "I call you."

Reflected candlelight flickered in the panes. Was it just her breath that moved it?

"I call you. . . ."

Maybe it was the dark, or the quiet, or the flickering light, but behind her reflection, she thought she saw the outline of a low, hulking shadow. It was gone as soon as she glimpsed it. Had it been on the outside or inside of the glass?

Eliza shuddered. Her hip bumped the table, making the candle waver.

Don't be silly. Ghosts can't hurt you.

She tried to swallow, but her throat felt dry and tight, like a crumpled paper straw. "I call you. . . ."

And then, in the darkness behind her, something growled.

Eliza whirled around.

Crouched a few feet away, near enough that it could close the gap in one lunge, was a wolf.

A massive, charcoal gray wolf.

The biggest wolf Eliza had ever seen anywhere.

Even in a crouch, its face was level with hers. She stared straight into its snarling maw and burning gold eyes.

She recognized those eyes.

They were the same inhuman eyes that had stared at her from the stormy backyard.

A burst of triumph—*the summoning had worked!*—seeped away in a swell of terror. She was staring into the jaws of a wolf. A huge, hulking, snarling wolf.

Then, to make things even worse, the wolf spoke.

"You have something that belongs to me," it growled.

Its voice was low. Soft. Disused. It made Eliza's skin crawl with a thousand icy spiders, all of them screaming, *Run away!*

But if she ran, she would be letting fear take control. No. She needed to think. She needed to keep the berry safe. She needed to keep the wolf here, in hopes that someone else would come to help her.

She needed to *stall*.

"Wh-what do you mean?" she stammered, closing her fist around the berry.

"I smell it." The wolf's voice grew deeper still. It stepped

closer, its huge paws rasping on the floor. "Just like I can smell your fear."

"Oh. I've *heard* that animals can smell fear," said Eliza, her own voice high and trembling. "I've just never heard it from the horse's mouth before. Or from the wolf's mouth, I mean!" Sheesh, she sounded like Mr. Carroll. Panic was making her goofy.

Subtly as she could, she edged sideways, putting distance between them. But the wolf caught this. It tracked each movement, its head lowering, its powerful body twitching. Ready to spring.

"Give me the fruit," it growled.

Eliza's mind whirled. What *was* this creature? A ghost? A werewolf? A berry-eating human? Did it even matter? She gripped the berry. If she could reach the greenhouse doors, she might be able to escape—or at least to scream for help.

"Why should I give it to you?" She took another sideways step.

"Otherwise," growled the wolf, "I will be forced to *take* it."

With those words, Eliza's fear won. She dove to the right, around the end of a table. The wolf charged after her. Eliza felt a freezing gust sweep over her, as though the wolf itself was made of ice.

She tore down the row, her shoes pounding the floor. The wolf coursed easily, silently, after her. She had to delay. She had to outmaneuver it somehow.

Desperately, Eliza grabbed the edge of one table and swung herself beneath. The wolf lunged after her, its broad body knocking the table out of place. That table crashed into the next one, setting it wobbling. Two plants toppled from its surface, along with Eliza's burning candle—which fell directly into a pile of dry leaves.

The candle glass shattered.

Eliza heard the crackle of leaves catching fire. She saw the flare as the leaves burst into flame, and then another flare as the fire reached a pile of cardboard boxes. She scurried beneath the next table.

The wolf paused, giving the spreading fire one swift glance. It turned back toward Eliza, hunched its shoulders, and sprang.

Eliza shot to her feet. The table above her crashed down onto its side, sending an avalanche of potted plants into the wolf's path. The wolf snarled, its heavy body smashing through the plants and striking the barricade of the tabletop. Eliza couldn't stall any longer. She raced along the row, straight toward the doors.

The air of the greenhouse was thickening with heat and smoke. Her eyes stung. Beneath her own gasping breaths, she could hear the fire, crackling and snapping as it spread. She was two steps from the doors when a dark hulk leaped into her path.

Eliza reeled back.

The wolf had landed inches away. It crouched between her and the doors, its golden eyes glimmering with reflected flames. Its lips curled back, revealing rows of long, jagged teeth.

"Give me the fruit," it commanded, in a growl that made every hair on Eliza's body tremble.

The hand holding the berry shook.

There was no escape. She was caught between a wolf and a spreading fire.

She'd thought she could do this all alone.

She'd been wrong.

Wrong.

Wrong.

Helpless, hopeless, she lifted the berry toward the wolf's glinting jaws.

A piercing BEEEEEEEEEEP blared through the greenhouse.

Eliza flinched, raising both hands to her ears. The wolf flinched, too. As they huddled there, pinned in place by the noise, a blast of cold water filled the air. It shot down from the spigots covering the ceiling. It stung Eliza's eyes and soaked through her clothes. Coughing, half-blinded, she heard the fire hissing out.

Someone switched on the lights.

Eliza pushed a hank of soaked hair out of her eyes.

Between the open greenhouse doors stood her mother and Leif, and the Carrolls and Tommy in dog form. Mr. Carroll rose onto his hind legs and pawed a switch on the wall. The blaring fire alarm died. The sprinkler system gave a final splutter.

Moggie barreled into the greenhouse. She charged straight to Eliza, licking the water off her arms and snuffling at the hand that still held the red berry, safe and sound. Then, growling loudly, she wheeled around to face the wolf.

But the wolf wasn't there.

Hunched in front of Eliza, holding the lapels of his dripping black coat, was a man. The man she had spoken to in the shop. His broad hat and plastic sunglasses were gone, so Eliza could clearly see his sharp-featured face, his drenched black hair. His burning yellow eyes.

"It's you," she whispered.

Eliza tricked the culprit into comi back! But wait, who IS this guy? Turn to page 257

18

THE GHOST STOOD VERY still. Water dripped from the cuffs of his coat. In his squelchy human state, he looked far less intimidating than a moment ago. He looked wet and uncomfortable and *real*.

Nudging Moggie aside, Eliza stepped closer. The man watched her, keeping perfectly still. He didn't even move when Eliza reached out and, very gently, touched his arm.

It was solid. Wet. Warm.

Alive.

"You're not a ghost," Eliza whispered.

"No," the man murmured back in that low, old-fashioned voice. She should have recognized it before. "I am not."

"But . . ." Eliza looked up into his flickering yellow eyes. "You're not really *human*, either. Are you?"

"No," said the man again. "Not anymore."

Eliza's mother seemed to snap out of an observational trance. She charged into the greenhouse, wrapping an arm around Eliza and planting herself firmly in the man's path. "I take it you're the one who's been terrorizing us," she said, the hedge-trimmer voice out in full force. "*Stealing* from us."

The man's face seemed to flicker. Not just to flicker, but to shift—becoming longer and more pointed in places, flatter and darker in others. When he spoke, Eliza could see the flash of a wolf's long teeth.

"It is you who have stolen from *me*," he growled. His burning eyes swiveled to Leif, who was trying to hide behind the trio of dogs. "It was you who came to my home. Who uprooted the plant. Who brought it here, endangering all of its kind, endangering all of *my* kind, endangering the world at large."

By the time he was finished, his voice was a roar. His form had shifted into something between wolf and human, hulking, huge, and terrifying.

Leif let out a squeak and dove behind Mr. Carroll.

"All right, everyone," said Eliza's mother much less sharply. She held up both hands. "Let's proceed calmly and logically. First things first. Who are you?"

"My name is William," the wolf-man said through clenched fangs. "Or it used to be."

"Can we assume that you have the missing plant?"

Slowly, William opened his coat, revealing a shaggy chest and a bundle of gold leaves thrusting up from an inner pocket. "I do. And I will bring it safely home, or destroy every trace of it."

Eliza swallowed. The Carrolls shifted nervously.

"And where is 'home'?" Eliza's mother went on.

"The island where the plant was taken from, of course."

"Hang on." Leif's head poked up behind the bulldog. "You're telling us you *lived* on that little deserted island? All by yourself?"

"No." William's face was shifting again, the canine muzzle shortening, although his teeth remained long and sharp. "With my family. Others like myself."

"How long have you inhabited the island?" Eliza's mother asked.

"For a very long time." William's voice softened slightly. "We live on fish and game, and on the fruit of this plant."

"So you all eat the fruit," said her mother. "And you all . . . *change*?"

William smiled a fanged half-smile. "The longer one

eats of the fruit, the more powerful one becomes. With that power comes size. Strength. Control. I myself can change at will, as you see. Unless I am temporarily overcome," he added, pouring a dribble of water out of one sleeve.

Eliza looked at that old-fashioned coat, and then at William's shifting, inhuman, ageless face. "How old *are* you?"

"In human or dog years?" boomed Mr. Carroll.

"Oh, Win!" giggled Mrs. Carroll.

Eliza's mother rolled her eyes.

But William gazed steadily down at her. "I am older than even I know."

"Will that happen to us?" the shaggy brown mutt asked, in Tommy's anxious voice. "Will we get more powerful over time, too?"

"How much of the fruit have you eaten?"

"Um . . . one berry?"

William's teeth flashed again. "Happily for all of us, the effects of an amount that small should wear off quickly. Perhaps within a week."

The Carrolls let out yips of joy. The Boston terrier snuggled up to the bulldog and gave a relieved sigh.

"A single berry is nothing compared to eating the fruit for a lifetime." William closed his coat gently over the golden leaves. "This plant is not just part of our diet and key to our survival. It is at the root of our way of life. You might even call it sacred to us. We have our own name for it: *Canis mirabilis.*"

"Ah!" Eliza's mother brightened. "A play on the Latin phrase *annus mirabilis*, miraculous year. Miraculous *dog*. Very clever!"

"When you stole this plant from us"—William leveled another burning yellow glare at Leif—"I was compelled to follow you and retrieve it. If I did not, the effects would be disastrous."

Eliza's mother cocked her head. "How so?"

His eyes flashed to her. "You know *how so*. My family would be hunted and captured. Our island raided. Its ecology destroyed. The plant brought to the wider world, where it would be cultivated, studied, sold to the wealthiest among you, used by those who had enough money and power to control others or to enrich themselves further. It would mean destruction and chaos."

Eliza pictured armies of wolves racing into battle, and then tubby, pampered, ageless dogs in gleaming city penthouses. She pictured a little forested island turned to a stripped chunk of rock. Maybe it was because she was still soaking wet, but suddenly her entire body felt cold.

"Like Tibbles the cat," whispered Tommy.

"*Cat?*" Mrs. Carroll hopped up and looked eagerly around, then seemed to catch herself. "Oh. I'm *so* sorry. Hunting instinct."

"Go on, Tommy," Eliza's mother commanded.

"Um . . ." The brown mutt blinked around at them all. "Stephens Island is this little island near New Zealand. It was the

163

only place in the world that was home to the Stephens Island wren. In the 1890s, people started building a lighthouse there, and a few ships' cats got loose on the island—people used to think it was just Tibbles, the lighthouse keeper's cat, but there were probably others—and in less than a year, the wrens were extinct. The cats killed them. And then, because the cats reproduced like crazy without any larger predators, people had to start shooting the feral cats until all of *them* were dead."

"Ew," said Eliza sadly.

"Yeah, but it proves the point." The mutt tried to shrug. "When you bring a new thing into an ecosystem—even if it's just one plant, or one cat—the effects can be huge."

Everyone was still.

"We are a small group, living on a small island," said William at last. "We are part of our own contained and balanced world. But with just one seed of *Canis mirabilis* . . . any one of you could be Tibbles the cat."

Quiet settled over the greenhouse once more.

"Well, I'm not interested in being Tibbles the cat," boomed Mr. Carroll at last. "I've always been more of a dog person myself!"

"Yes," agreed Mrs. Carroll. "William, if we had known all this, we would never have brought that plant here."

Eliza looked up at her mother. "Mom?" she whispered. "Do you think he's right?"

Her mother closed her eyes. "You know, I fully expect to wake up tomorrow morning and discover that all of this was an absurd dream, because there is simply no way in the real world that I am discussing returning an undiscovered plant with transformational powers to the island that it came from with a bunch of *dogs in pajamas.*" She opened her eyes again. "But I am. And as disappointed as I might be, scientifically, to have to say this . . . Leif should sail you and your plant home."

Leif, who had started to look calmer, stiffened up again. "What? I don't want to go all the way back to that creepy little island."

"And *I* don't *want* to go to the authorities about your plant poaching," said the bulldog. "But sometimes we have to do what we don't want to do."

Leif rasped something under his breath, but he didn't argue.

"We should get you on your way!" said Mrs. Carroll brightly. "Hurry, everyone!"

Everybody burst into action.

Mr. Carroll shut himself in the basement and jogged back out minutes later on two feet. Leif called his crew and grumpily told them to get ready for another long trip. Mrs. Carroll and Tommy sniffed around the greenhouse, surveying the fire damage, which turned out to be quite minimal. And Moggie trotted around everyone's feet, tripping people and licking their ankles.

Eliza found her mother at the back door, gazing out into the night. She touched her arm. "Are you okay?"

Her mother let out a long, tight breath. "No. I would

not say that *okay* is what I am." She looked down at Eliza. "You're a researcher, so perhaps you'll understand. Do you know how it feels to discover something that clashes so completely with everything else you believe that it shakes those beliefs to their foundations? That it makes you wonder how many of your beliefs are based on incorrect premises? Or on nothing at all?"

"Actually, I usually feel the opposite," said Eliza. "The things I discover just give me more possibilities to believe in." She leaned her head on her mother's shoulder. "But I guess that just means I need to keep looking."

Her mother gave her a quick squeeze. "Good plan."

"All right! All aboard that's going aboard!" shouted Mr. Carroll, hurrying toward the van. Leif slumped reluctantly after him. Eliza's mother, Tommy, and Mrs. Carroll followed them into the garage.

William glided past Eliza, his long black coat sweeping the floor. Then he stopped sharply and turned to face her. Even in the darkness, his eyes seemed to catch and burn with light.

Eliza felt the same icy gust that she'd felt before: the sense that told her there were supernatural powers here. Or maybe just super*natural* powers.

"Oh," she said. "I almost forgot. But I guess you didn't." Shivering, she held out the red berry on her palm.

William took it with fingers that were long and sharp-nailed, but very careful. Eliza watched the berry disappear between his teeth. "Thank you, Eliza," he said in that deep, old-fashioned voice. "I have something to return to you as well." Reaching inside his coat, he pulled out Eliza's research notebook.

"Really?" Eliza hesitated. "I thought you had to take all evidence of the plant."

William smiled. His teeth looked less vicious now. "I believe I can trust you with this secret. And I would hate for you to lose so much spectral research."

Eliza's cheeks burned. She grabbed the damp notebook, looking away. Was he mocking her? All her research had come to nothing, and he knew it.

"The world is full of wonders," William said very softly. "This should give you more reason, not less, to believe that." He touched her shoulder so lightly that she barely felt it. "Farewell, Eliza."

He climbed into the back of the van. Then Mr. Carroll, a wolf-man, and one grumpy sailor whooshed out of the garage and away into the night.

Does this mean the case is solved now? Turn to page 262.

THE NEXT DAY AT Carrolls' Gardens was very quiet.
Eliza and her mother, Tommy, and the Carrolls
went silently about their usual work. They had promised
not to talk about William or the plant, and suddenly it
seemed like there was nothing else to talk about. So they
didn't.

Eliza and her mother ate a muted dinner in their
room. Afterward, instead of reading ghost stories, Eliza
played mindless games on her tablet until little explod-
ing candies piled up behind her eyelids every time she
blinked. She went to bed feeling heavy and empty at the
same time.

But in the middle of the night, something woke her.

Eliza opened her eyes.

The room was still. Her mother snored softly in the
other bed. From somewhere nearby, there came a creak.

Eliza swung her feet to the floor. Instead of curiosity or excitement, all she felt was annoyance. Something had woken her. She was going to find it and make it *shut up*.

She grabbed her mother's flashlight—who cared if ghosts didn't like flashlights? Right now, she didn't like ghosts much herself—and stalked out into the hall.

The beam bounced along the empty corridor. Just ahead of her, the attic door shifted on its broken hinges.

Creeeak. Of course. That was all it was. A broken door shifting in the breeze.

Eliza turned, ready to stomp back to bed. She couldn't wait to be back in her own house, where there were no stupid broken doors trying to trick you, or—

Wait. Eliza halted. A breeze?

She guided the flashlight along the hallway again.

The first door stood slightly open.

Eliza slunk nearer.

Light from the street filtered through the room's dirty window. And that window was slightly open, too. A whisper of night air rushed over its sill, fluttering the hem of her T-shirt.

More carefully now, Eliza scanned the hallway. The attic door swung again, almost like an invisible hand was opening it for her. Eliza tiptoed through it, past the litter of empty chemical bottles, up the scorched stairs.

The attic was empty.

Eliza made doubly sure, slicing every corner and shadow with the flashlight. No movement. No dark-cloaked figures. She was about to thump back down the steps when her flashlight glanced over something sitting on a trunk—the half-dusted trunk she had noticed before.

It was a small glass jar.

Inside the jar, glinting like marbles or cinnamon candies, was something red.

Eliza dropped to her knees and grabbed the jar.

Berries. Familiar red berries. Several of them.

But . . . *how?* How had they gotten here? Who would be stupid and stubborn enough to do this? And why?

The questions piled up like fuel on a fire. And, suddenly, she was *furious*.

It was straight-up, full-on fury, like she'd felt when she'd spotted a couple of obnoxious boys from her grade smashing the jack-o'-lanterns of her five-year-old twin neighbors. She'd taken off down the street after the boys, screaming about what wastes of cellular activity they were, and hurling pieces of broken pumpkin after them. She'd actually beaned one boy right on the head. She'd felt feverish, and righteous, and almost out-of-control.

Gripping the jar, Eliza shot to her feet. She would destroy the fruits. And then she'd figure out who did this, and she'd bean *them* on the head.

It could be Tommy. This was the spot he'd used for his secret plant studies, after all. It would be pretty stupid of him to return to such an obvious place, and it seemed odd that Tommy—who understood the dangers—would steal the berries to begin with. So maybe it wasn't Tommy. Maybe his aunt and uncle had done it. The Carrolls had been willing to bend rules and keep secrets before. Or—maybe—maybe a certain obsessive gray-eyed botanist couldn't stand to let every trace of this plant disappear.

Eliza swallowed. All the more reason to destroy the evidence immediately.

She turned toward the attic steps.

But creaking up the stairs, with his own flashlight and a big duffel bag, was someone else.

Eliza and Leif both jumped.

"Geez!" said Leif, wide-eyed. "What are you doing up here, Eliza?"

"I heard something." Eliza tucked the jar behind her back. "What are *you* doing up here? I thought your boat would be way out in the ocean by now."

"The boat is." Leif held up his left hand, which was wadded in a knot of bandages. "I managed to slam my hand in a metal case just before we left the docks. Had to come back here, visit the ER, send the crew on without me."

"But William and the plant?" Eliza asked. "They're safe on board?"

"Of course." Leif swung his duffel bag to the floor and set the flashlight beside it. "Should be past Massachusetts by now." He sighed, scratching under his cap with one tattooed hand. "It was so late when I left the hospital, I didn't want to wake everyone, but I knew Win and Camila wouldn't mind if I climbed up the old fire escape and sacked out here." He grinned ruefully. "Sorry if I woke you. I'll let you get back to bed. I'm beat myself."

"It's okay." Eliza sidled past, keeping the jar behind her back. "Good night."

"Hey," said Leif. "What've you got there?"

Eliza would have darted down the stairs, but Leif stood in her path. "It's . . ." She hesitated. "Just something I found."

Leif's pale eyes focused on her face. "Hey! Is that from that plant? Did you steal those?"

"No!" Eliza exclaimed. "I found it up here. I was going to get rid of it."

Leif studied her. Eliza wasn't sure if she saw distrust or mere wariness in his eyes, but they seemed to grow even sharper. "Somebody must've been tempted," he said. "Just *one* of those berries could be worth a lot."

"Not worth risking the ecological balance of the whole world," said Eliza.

She sounded exactly like her mother, she realized. And exactly like Tommy, with his Tibbles the cat story.

The truth crashed over her. There was no way her mother or Tommy would have stolen these fruits. So that meant . . .

"Here." Leif held out his good hand. "Why don't you head down to bed, and I'll take care of those."

Eliza looked into his pale blue eyes.

Something cold lanced through her.

Dropping the flashlight, she lunged for the stairs. But Leif grabbed her in one ropy arm. His bandaged hand clamped over her mouth.

"Sorry, Eliza," he said. "I can't let you get rid of those berries when it took me so much work and two broken fingers to save them."

Eliza wrenched her head sideways far enough to see Leif's face.

"Yep." He gave another half-grin. "I'm actually pretty

pleased with how it all went. I had to wait until William was fast asleep, of course. Lucky for me, but unlucky for him, I used to make a living as a pickpocket. I got a handful of berries without him even twitching." Leif gave a raspy chuckle. "Then I needed a reason to get back ashore that wouldn't make the other guys suspicious, so I had to injure my own hand. But I've worked a lot of jobs between pick-pocketing and treasure hunting. I've been a stunt man. A pastry chef. A rodeo clown. And if *that* job taught me any-thing, it's how to create a distraction, and how to handle a little pain." He cough-laughed again. "I'm thinking it's time for another career change. Pickpocketing was small pota-toes. Now I'll pull off jewel heists. Bank robberies, maybe. Nobody's going to suspect a *dog*, right? I know they call them cat burglars, but I think it's time that a dog burglar has his day!" Leif stopped and shook his head. "Geez. I sound just like Win."

He closed his good hand around the jar in Eliza's fist. "Guess I'm like him in more ways than one. Just got some pots and soil from downstairs." He nodded at his duffel bag. "Once I plant the berries, I'll have a whole little rare plant store of my own."

With a sudden desperate writhe, Eliza broke out of Leif's grip. She ran, not toward the stairs, but toward one of the attic windows, still clutching the jar. Caught off guard, Leif scrambled after.

Eliza unlatched the sticky old window. She shoved the

pane upward. Outside, a tiny ledge ran around the edge of the turret's pointed tip. Four stories down, pavement gleamed beneath the streetlamps, damp and dark.

Leif grabbed her arm.

Eliza passed the jar to her free hand and thrust it through the window.

"Let go of me," she shouted, "or I'll drop this jar and smash it on the street!"

"Give me the jar," Leif said softly back, "or I'll push you straight out this window."

Terror froze the fire inside her. She had calculated wrong. Now she was pressed against the windowsill, half her body already leaning through it, with Leif blocking her only escape. There was nowhere to go. Nowhere except . . .

Before she could think twice, Eliza wriggled out the window.

Cool, dewy air swirled around her. It wasn't a windy night, but somehow the height made every breeze seem strong enough to shove her off her feet. She balanced on the narrow ledge, leaning back against the cold metal of the turret. The jar trembled in her hand.

"Now what?" asked Leif. "You going to sprout wings?"

Eliza scanned the street—the very distant street—below. No one was on the sidewalks. Businesses were dark and closed. She screamed anyway. "Help!" Wind ripped her voice away. "Somebody *help!*"

Leif put one leg through the window. "Give me that jar,

and maybe I'll help you back inside. Otherwise I'll climb out there after you."

Eliza glanced back at Leif's pale eyes. Then she sidled out of his reach. Every motion made her stomach flip. Any tiny mistake, any slip, any twitch, and she would plunge straight over the edge.

Leif sighed. "All right, then." He pulled his other leg through the window. "But I warn you: I've lived on a boat. I can balance on a wet two-inch rail."

Eliza shuffled sideways. One heel hit a dent in the ledge, and for a second, she swayed, her body wavering, her knees jerking with panic, before she managed to lean back and catch herself on the turret again.

Leif had moved out onto the ledge. "Only one of us is coming back through this window," he said, inching closer. "And it's going to be—"

But he stopped there.

His body jerked as though something had grabbed him from behind. He glanced over his shoulder.

Eliza heard a growl. *Two* growls.

Leif flew backward through the window.

There was a scuffling sound. More growls. A sharp *CRACK*.

Eliza threw out her arms, wobbling in place. The night air whipped through her hair.

A shaggy brown head popped through the window.

"Here!" The dog thrust out a paw. "Hold on!"

Gripping the jar with her other hand, Eliza grabbed hold. The dog tugged her through the open window and onto the attic floor, where Moggie was guarding Leif's unconscious form. A broken ceramic planter—one that Tommy must have clobbered him with—lay nearby.

Eliza flopped onto the floorboards. Moggie flung herself into Eliza's lap and covered her face with kisses.

"How did you know?" Eliza gasped, between slobbers. "Did you *smell* him or something?"

"It was Moggie," said Tommy. "She jumped onto my bed and nosed me until I got up. I guess she sensed that you needed a friend. Or two of them."

Eliza threw her arms around Moggie, who panted happily in her ear. Then she threw her arms around Tommy, who stiffened up like an ironing board, but who couldn't help wagging his tail.

• • •

They decided to save time on explanations by getting them all over with at once.

After binding Leif with so many ropes that he looked like a huge cocoon, they woke Eliza's mother, trooped down to the Carrolls' apartment, and got the Carrolls out of bed. The Carrolls had drawn thick curtains over the windows, so they were already in human form, but they all waited while Tommy shut himself in the bathroom to change shape and pull some clothes on. Then Tommy and Eliza sat down on the couch, with Moggie stretched protectively across their feet, and told the whole story.

Mrs. Carroll was horrified. Mr. Carroll was furious. Eliza's mother got so distraught that Eliza had to coach her through a round of full-body stretches.

After they had burned the berries in a metal pan until nothing was left but some oily soot, Eliza's mother went to call the police. Mr. Carroll headed to the attic to guard Leif until they arrived. Mrs. Carroll fluttered away to brew herbal tea.

Eliza and Tommy and Moggie were left alone in the leafy living room. Moggie yawned and stretched herself across their ankles. Eliza felt tired, too. Tired and—finally—safe.

"Um . . . ," said Tommy softly, at last. "I think I might be done studying plants for a while. Botany is *dangerous*."

Eliza nodded. "I've always said it: The natural world is a messy, terrifying place. The *super*natural world is much safer."

Tommy nodded back. "It sure sounds super."

It was just the kind of stupid joke Mr. Carroll would have made. Eliza giggled. Tommy snorted. Then they both laughed out loud, cracking each other up again. Finally, exhausted, they flopped back against the cushions.

"Maybe I'll try that instead," said Tommy. "Paranormal research, I mean. If you don't mind."

"No," said Eliza quickly. "I wouldn't mind at all. It would be really nice to have someone to talk to about it."

"Okay then." Tommy smiled down at the floor. "Good."

There was another moment of quiet.

"So ... um ...," Tommy spoke up again. "What are some of your favorite ghost stories?"

Eliza wriggled back into the cushions. "Have you heard of the Woman in Black?"

She told that story and then another and another, while the moon outside the curtains dissolved into the brightening sky, and Moggie, snoring deeply, drooled onto their socks.

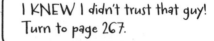

I KNEW I didn't trust that guy! Turn to page 267.

THE ISLAND HAD THREE things: darkness, solitude, and quiet.

One old wooden boat bobbed in its cove. On shore, there was no sign of life at all—nothing but a single dark figure gliding up a slope, away from the water. It paused to lift a hand to the boat. Then it turned, pulling its cloak of shadows around itself, and stepped into the trees. In moments it was out of sight.

The figure walked on, through woods where strange birds called to each other, where trees no one else had ever seen shushed and rustled, until it reached a grove of golden leaves and gleaming red berries.

There the figure crouched and scraped a hole in the soil. It pulled a slightly battered seedling out of its coat and set it inside. It patted the soil gently around its roots.

It was just rising to its feet again when, from beyond the next hill, there came a howl. That howl was joined by another and another and another, a chorus of happy, haunting voices singing a song without words. Welcoming him home.

The figure smiled. His lengthening teeth glittered in the moonlight. Then he dropped to all fours and raced off over the hill, his own howl joining in the song.

Hey, this reminds me of that spooky prologue! Turn to page 268.

MYSTERY CREATION ZONE

BY QUINTON JOHNSON

CONTENTS
MYSTERY CREATION ZONE SHORTCUTS

MYSTERY CREATION ZONE

THE END: CRACKING THE CASE

MYSTERY CREATION ZONE

CAN YOU KEEP A SECRET?

Secrets.

That's the first word of this novel, which makes sense, because it's a mystery story—and mystery stories are all about secrets. That's probably why mysteries are so popular: People love to find out about what others are trying to hide. You might know the feeling. If a friend of yours is keeping a secret from you, sometimes you get to the point where you can't *stand* it anymore. You have to find out what the answer is, even if you have to *beg* your friend to tell you.

The fun thing about writing a mystery is that it's the *author* who knows the secret. Your readers want you to tell it to them, but you're not going to ... at least not right away. First, you give them little clues about your secret ... then you tell them a bit more, and a bit more ... until they're *begging* to hear the rest! They start turning the pages faster and faster and can't put the story down, until they finally discover what you've been hiding.

Mysteries can be about small secrets (someone is stealing candy) or huge secrets (the government is trying to hide the aliens who have come to Earth). Sometimes a mystery starts with one secret, but then more and more secrets get revealed along the way. (While trying to figure out who stole the candy, we accidentally discover secret aliens!)

But it doesn't matter if your secret is big or small. The trick to a good mystery is all in *how* you tell it to your reader. One . . . small . . . clue . . . at . . . a . . . time.

Like most stories, mysteries have a **beginning, a middle,** and an **end.** Usually, it goes something like this:

The Beginning: *Setting the Scene*
A mystery is discovered, and a character decides to solve it.

The Middle: *The Investigation*
The character tries to solve the mystery.

The End: *Cracking the Case*
The mystery is solved!

Ideas for a mystery might come from anywhere—hopefully you'll get a few ideas while reading this book! If you have a good idea for a setting where the mystery takes place, or for a detective character to solve it, you can get started right away and see where your imagination takes you.

But before you get too far, there's something else important to know. Something that makes writing mysteries different from writing other kinds of stories. Something . . . strange.

When you *read* a mystery story, you read it in order from beginning to end, just like any other story. But when you *write* a mystery story, you need to decide what the **end** is going to be while you're still writing the **beginning.** Even though your *reader* won't know the big secret behind your mystery until the end, *you* already have to know it when you're just getting started. It's only once you know the secret that you can start to give your reader tiny clues, surprise them with mysterious events, and plan out a satisfying story where all the pieces fit together and make sense.

Weird, right? So how do you actually do that? How do you come up with a mysterious secret and then keep the reader wondering what it is for a whole story? In the pages that follow, we'll give you lots of advice for how to do exactly that, plus some games to help you practice before you start writing. For now the most important question to ask yourself is: **Can you keep a secret?**

If you can do that, then you can write a mystery!

HOW DOES THE MYSTERY CREATION ZONE WORK?

In the Mystery Creation Zone, we'll explain the basics of how to build a mystery, and give you tips for keeping the audience on the edge of their seat. As you read through, you'll see three different kinds of entries:

Detective's Notebook. When you write a mystery, you're creating a puzzle for the reader, and the Detective's Notebook entries are there to help you keep track of all the pieces. You'll learn about choosing a setting and characters, how to invent a mystery of your own, and how the detective will dig up clues to finally crack the case.

Mystery Writer Challenge. The mind of a mystery writer works a little differently from other people's. A mystery writer needs to practice looking at the mysterious side of life, where clues and conspiracies might be lurking around every corner, and learn how to tell secrets in the most suspenseful way possible. Each Mystery Writer Challenge will offer tips, games, and activities to try at home to help you think and write like an experienced mystery writer.

Idea Storm. This is where you create a mysterious puzzle of your own! We'll give you tips to brainstorm ideas and build your own mystery story.

Besides that, we want you to keep in mind two big things:

First, **your story is not going to start out perfect.** No mystery has ever been written perfectly on a first draft. Ever. You might not come up with your best idea for a clue until you're almost done, and you'll have to go back and add it to the middle of the story. Or maybe it's not until the fourth time you've read a paragraph that you realize the perfect way to make the setting sound mysterious and exciting. That's great! Go back and make it as good as it can be!

All writers go back and rewrite their work—*especially* mystery writers. When Jacqueline West was building *Digging Up Danger* out of Phoebe's idea, she totally rewrote the last five chapters over and over again until the ending was as exciting as possible.

If you're writing with a pencil and paper, one way to make this easier for yourself is to **skip lines** so there's room on the page to cross things out and add new ideas. For example, if you wrote some sentences you think sound a little boring, add new details to make them more interesting (and mysterious):

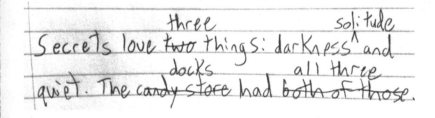

Jacqueline West always writes her first draft by hand in a journal for this very reason!

Second, give yourself **PERMISSION TO GET WEIRD.** Maybe you've read a lot of mystery books, watched tons of mystery shows on TV, and have a pretty good idea of how they usually go. It's worth remembering that the most memorable, shocking, amazing mysteries are WEIRD. The secrets in them are so WEIRD the audience never sees them coming. In fact, the whole idea of a "mystery" used to be WEIRD. Nobody had ever written a real mystery story until a guy named Edgar Allan Poe came along and wrote the first ones ever. They were unlike anything that had been written before (a *whole story* about a detective looking for clues and trying to find out a secret?), but soon mysteries were one of the most popular kinds of stories in the world. Sometimes the very best ideas sound WEIRD . . . at first.

And sure, maybe you'll write down a WEIRD idea and then decide, "Nah. That one's too strange. I don't like it." That's fine, too! You can always cross it out, erase it, or delete it. But you'll never know for sure how it sounds until you try writing it, no matter how WEIRD.

 See that ? Every time it shows up, it's a clue that means it's the end of the section. If you got here by flipping forward from page 4, flip back and keep reading!

Yeah! Read carefully and see if you can figure out the terrifying secret I planted in my mystery story.

 Terrifying secret? What have you gotten me into here, Phoebe?

THE BEGINNING: SETTING THE SCENE

🔍 DETECTIVE'S NOTEBOOK: MYSTERIOUS PROLOGUE

Secrets love three things . . .

How puzzling! What was happening in that chapter? Who were those mysterious people? What was up with that one shadow sneaking into the night?

If you can get your reader asking these kinds of questions right at the beginning of a mystery story, you're off to a great start. Already, you've got them *begging* to know the secret you're hiding.

This kind of beginning is called a **mysterious prologue:** You give your readers hints about some secrets that are going to be in the book, in order to get them excited for your mystery. How do you write a mysterious prologue like this in your story? Well, this is one of those cases where you have to decide what the **end** is going to be *before* you can write the **beginning.** So we're going to have to come back to this at the *very end* of this book.

Sorry to keep you in suspense! But just like in a mystery story, we can't give away all the secrets right at the start.

✏️ MYSTERY WRITER CHALLENGE: SUSPENSEFUL SIMILES

. . . a turret with a top like a metal witch's hat.

A mystery writer wants to set the mood for the reader at the very beginning, to let them know this is going to be a suspenseful, mysterious story. One way to do that is with a **simile.** In a simile, the author compares a person or thing in the story to something else—usually to something unexpected.

For example, let's take the turret in our story (a "turret" is a small tower coming off the top of a building). If you wanted to set a funny mood, you might say "a turret like a giant banana." Or if you wanted the building to sound grand and beautiful, you could say "a turret like the top of a proud old castle."

But the author of this mystery didn't describe the turret in those ways. She chose a very specific way to describe it, which fit the mysterious mood she wanted: *"a turret with a top like a metal witch's hat."* You're going to see a lot more of these similes as you keep reading. Be on the lookout for a chandelier that hangs *"like a big glass spider,"* a hallway *"dark as wet ink,"* and many more.

This brings us to a game called "Make it Mysterious," which will help you add a little mystery to your own life, while also giving you good practice for writing suspenseful similes. You can start by looking at objects around you. For example, let's say the television is off. How could you compare the boring dark TV to something mysterious? Is it "dark as a musty tomb?" Or can you see your face reflected in it "like a ghost peering in at the world of the living?"

You can also come up with similes for people. Are your teacher's fingernails painted "red like her fingers had been dipped in blood"? Is your next-door neighbor sitting on his front steps "as silent as a wolf stalking his prey"?

If you get in the habit of comparing normal, everyday things to weird, mysterious things, you'll have a lot of good practice for when you write a mystery.

 DETECTIVE'S NOTEBOOK: MYSTERY SETTING

Do you want to write a story set in a creepy, mysterious place, where secrets lurk around every corner? Are there locked basements, secret passageways, peculiar objects, and strange people who seem like they're trying to hide something?

Or maybe you want to write about a totally normal place you know a lot about, like your neighborhood or your school. At least, maybe this place *seems* normal, until you take a closer look and start uncovering all the weird secrets hiding there. . . .

The **setting** for your mystery—where and when it takes place—can be anywhere. If *you* think it would be an interesting place for a mystery, then it probably is! One tip to make your job easier is to think about a setting where there are *lots of people around*. This could be a plant store, a school, a beach, a train, a party at an old mansion, a starship full of ninja scientists . . . anywhere your imagination can come up with. The more people you have in your setting, the more secrets there will be to uncover, and the more suspects there will be to investigate (more on that later).

Once you've decided on a setting, it's a good idea to think carefully about the characters who spend time there. What kind of people (or animals, or imaginary creatures) do you want in your mystery story? Then it's important to imagine the setting with your **five senses:** What can you see, hear, smell, touch, and taste there? Check out the Mystery Setting organizer on page 196 for an example of what we mean.

As you look it over, you'll notice lots of details about Carrolls' Gardens, the exotic plant store where *Digging Up Danger* takes place. You may also notice that one box has been left blank: "Is there anything in this setting you're keeping *secret* from the reader?" We didn't leave it blank because there's no secret in Carrolls' Gardens. There is.

MYSTERY SETTING

Setting Carolls' Gardens—an exotic plant store

Who spends time there?
Mr. and Mrs. Caroll (the owners), their nephew Tommy, their dog
Moggie, Prof. Stahl (a scientist studying plants), her daughter Eliza,
lots of customers.

Use your senses to describe this place on a normal day:

What you hear:
The bell above the front door
Mr. Caroll's deep voice
Mrs. Caroll's high voice
Creaky stairs

What you smell:
Thousands of plants!
Leaves and flowers

What you taste:
Spicy jollof rice

What you touch:
Leaves, branches, cold air
by the attic door

What you see:
Lots and lots of green leaves.
Bright flowers   Colorful rugs

A turret with the top like a metal
witch's hat

Is there anything in this setting you're keeping secret from the reader?

We left it blank because it's a *secret*. If you want to find out what it is, you'll need to keep reading.

📖 MYSTERY WRITER CHALLENGE: SETTING THE SCENE

Once you've used your *five senses* to think about the setting, the next step for a writer is just as important: **setting the scene** for the reader so that they feel like they're actually there. How do you do that?

Here's an example: In Carrolls' Gardens, we already know from the Mystery Setting organizer on page 196 that you see "lots and lots of green leaves" and smell "thousands of plants." But in the novel it doesn't just say "Eliza saw lots and lots of green leaves and smelled thousands of plants." Instead, it says:

> *First came the smell. It was a deep, damp, leafy smell, the smell of thousands of living things breathing and bloom-ing. Then came the rush of color: emerald green, jade green, black-green. Green so thick and bright you could practically hear it. Green in the racks and shelves and tables full of plants, on the walls and windows climbing with vines, in the lily pads floating on the indoor pond.*

The writer has given us LOTS of details, telling us EXACTLY what the setting looks, sounds, feels, smells, and tastes like. Even if you're brainstorming ideas on a Mystery Setting organizer, when it comes time to write the story, you've got to be so detailed you make the reader feel like they're standing right there in the setting, soaking it in with *all five senses.*

In fact, this brings us to a challenge! It's a game to help you practice describing your setting with LOTS of details. We call it "Deduce the Setting." Take a look at the following two descriptions and see if you can guess what the settings are:

1. The breeze whipped across my face, and as I opened my mouth I could taste a hint of salt on the wind. The sand was sinking beneath my bare feet as I walked forward, squinting from the bright sunlight. In the distance, over the tan and white of the sand, I could just make out the yellow circle of a Frisbee, flying between two laughing children.

Did you get that one? Too easy? Here's another:

2. Screams. That's what I heard first, starting high up in the air, but then quickly rushing toward the

ground. All around me, however, families chattered happily, paying no attention to the noise, and moving with excitement in all directions. The smell of food drew me forward, with the thick, sugary scent of fried dough hovering close by.

Did you figure it out? Look on page 274 to check the answer.

You can try this out yourself: Give your friends and family a description of a setting *you* think up, *without actually saying what the setting is.* You can either write it down ahead of time or make it up on the spot. Either way, if you give them enough clues from the five senses, they should be able to guess what it is. When you write an actual story, of course, you probably aren't going to make the reader guess the setting—but this game is good practice for adding enough details to bring your setting to life.

IDEA STORM: CREATE A MYSTERY SETTING

What setting will you choose for *your* mystery story? Will it be a strange, mysterious setting with danger lurking around every corner? Or somewhere that seems like a totally normal place . . . at first?

Take a look at our Mystery Setting organizer on page 196, and make your own version to help you imagine your setting! Pay special attention to describing the setting with all five senses, and remember to think carefully about what characters spend time there. That will become very important later.

What kind of secrets will you hide in your setting? It can be a small secret (there's a big box of quarters hidden under the bed), a gigantic secret (there's a dangerous ray gun with mysterious powers hidden under the bed), or anything in between. This doesn't even have to be the *main* secret that starts off your mystery (we'll talk more about that very soon). More secrets just make for a more interesting, surprising setting, whatever they are.

Also, don't forget that you have PERMISSION TO GET WEIRD in imagining this setting. You can make it a very unusual place (even if the unusual part is a *secret* . . . for now).

MYSTERY WRITER CHALLENGE: KEEPING THE READER IN SUSPENSE

Eliza edged around the room. She backed away from a cluster of plants that looked like they might bite and skirted something with a speckled seed pod as long as her arm. She was bending down to sniff a wrinkly blue flower when, from somewhere nearby, there came a deep, ghostly moan.

This is a classic way to build **suspense** in a mystery story. Let's look closely at what the author is doing in this paragraph:

1. The character looks around the setting.
2. The author describes a few things the character sees there. There's some good, detailed description, but nothing too shocking.
3. Right at the very end, the author slips in one final detail that is weird ... mysterious ... chilling ... *what does it mean?*

This is a technique you can use in your own mystery story. Write a little bit about the setting, but then at the end of the paragraph, have the character notice something ... weird. The weird thing could be a clue or an unexpected person. Maybe you don't even tell the reader what the weird thing is right away. You make them keep turning pages instead. For example, Eliza keeps looking around. . . .

She peered into the leafy shadows. When she took a small step sideways, the moan came again, a little bit louder.

Things are getting weirder. The reader really wants to know what's happening . . . but the writer has a secret to tell. It's no fun telling a secret all at once, so we're going to take our time and have Eliza keep looking around.

Eliza crouched down to look.

There was no vent. There was something else.

Something else? What was it?

From the darkness beneath a rack of plants, a black blob with gleaming yellow eyes stared straight back at her.

Eliza yelped.

Okay, so in the end, it turned out to just be a dog. But that's part of the fun of writing a mystery story: Instead of writing "Eliza saw a dog. She was startled at first," you can tell the reader about it *slowly* . . . not giving away the secret that it's a dog until the very end . . . making the reader excitedly turn pages wondering "What is it? What's the secret?"

Doing this is called keeping the reader in **suspense.**

Sometimes, early on in the story, the secret might turn out to be something normal, like a dog. Then, a little while later, the characters will run into something much, much weirder than a dog. . . .

Here's a way to start practicing this yourself: It's a game we call "Keep 'Em in Suspense." Find some friends or family members and get them to listen while you tell a short story following the steps below. You could write something down ahead of time, or just make it up in your head as you go along. Either way, to help set the right mood, you might talk in a low voice, or a whisper, and go *slowly*, like you're telling a mysterious secret.

1. Start by describing the setting. It can be a real place or an imaginary one. For example: "There was a supermarket on the corner. It was an old building, and a little small, but it was always full of people buying groceries."

2. Give a few more details about the setting. The details shouldn't be too shocking yet; just tell everyone a little more about the setting using your five senses: "Everyone especially loved the produce section. There was always fresh fruit and delicious vegetables, and in the fall you could smell the apples the second you walked in the store. They came from an orchard right outside of town."

3. Finally, add a *weird* detail that will make your listener wonder "What is it?" "One day the manager came in early to set up, when he noticed something odd. The apples were dripping something. It looked purple."

What was dripping? Were the apples so rotten their insides changed color? Or was it paint? What kind of maniac would paint an apple?

For now, you don't even need to decide on the answer! If you can keep your audience in **suspense,** wanting to know what will happen next, then you're getting in good practice for writing a mystery. If they ask you "What was it?" you can always say "You'll have to wait until I'm done writing my story to find out!"

Here's a quick bonus: During this challenge, you might be describing some WEIRD things. It would be repetitive to use the word *weird* over and over again, so here are some other words that mean the same thing, which you could use instead:

Weird	So weird it's funny	So weird it's scary
abnormal	absurd	creepy
bizarre	far-fetched	eerie
curious	kooky	freaky
odd	ludicrous	ominous
peculiar	outlandish	spooky
strange	preposterous	uncanny
unusual	wacky	unearthly

In fact, you can practice speaking these words out loud in real life any time you want to say that something is "weird." You'll be needing them a lot in a mystery story, so you might as well get used to saying them.

Once you have a setting, it's time to start thinking about the **mystery** you want to put there. How do you do it? There's no one correct way, but we have an easy place to start:

Think about your setting, and then think about something that is either MISSING from that setting, or something WEIRD that DOESN'T BELONG there.

In a classic mystery story, the missing thing might be something that was stolen (the diamonds are missing from the museum!), and the weird thing that doesn't belong might be a murder (how was the murderer able to strike on the middle of the basketball court without anyone seeing what happened?). But your mystery can be *much, much weirder than that* if you want. The thing that's missing might be all the water from the swimming pool . . . or a whole Ferris wheel from the amusement park. The weird thing that doesn't belong might be a tiger in a restaurant . . . or an alien spaceship on the school playground. *Anything* weird or missing in the setting can be the starting point for your mystery.

For example, in *Digging Up Danger* we have a couple of WEIRD things that DON'T BELONG:

- First, Eliza is sure she's seen signs of a ghost: mysterious figures that seem to vanish, unexplained sounds, peculiar shadows . . .

206

- Second, there are those incredibly rare plants, which even Professor Stahl has never seen before. Plants this rare are WEIRD, even in a plant store.

Are there really ghosts lurking around the building, and if so, what do they want? Is there any connection between the ghosts and the weird plants? The only way to find out will be to solve the **mystery**!

✏️ MYSTERY WRITER CHALLENGE: MAKING UP A MYSTERY

Want to get in some practice making up mysteries before you settle on one for your story? Try this game called "Puzzling Picture":

Take a look at the picture on page 208. Somewhere in this picture is a secret. Or several secrets, to be precise. Sure, it might look like an ordinary classroom . . . but something isn't quite right. There are some things in this scene that don't belong. Look carefully to see if you can pick out what's WEIRD here, and try to count how many WEIRD things you see.

Next, make up your own! Draw a picture of a setting and include as many details as possible. Then either add something WEIRD that DOESN'T BELONG, or decide on something MISSING that you would normally find there. Show your picture to your friends and family, and see if they can guess the mystery!

See page 274 for the answer.

Also, when some writers come up with a mystery, they enjoy saying it out loud in as mysterious a way as possible. For instance, they'll say "It's the case of the tiger in the restaurant!" or "It's the case of the missing Ferris wheel!" Then they'll sing "Dun dun DUUUUUUUN!" to sound extra mysterious. We're not saying YOU have to do that. We're just letting you know that SOME writers like to do it.

⚡ IDEA STORM: MAKE UP A MYSTERY

Think about your own setting and decide what mystery you want to put there! You can brainstorm ideas by drawing a setting, then choosing something that's MISSING or something WEIRD that DOESN'T BELONG there.

If you already came up with a "secret" on your Mystery Setting organizer (see page 196), the mystery might have something to do with that. (Maybe the quarters under the bed are missing . . . or maybe the ray gun opened a portal to outer space and made a comet appear in the backyard. Nobody can figure out where the comet came from!) But you can also *save* that secret for another time—it might come in handy later in the story.

Finally, don't forget that you have permission to make your mystery as WEIRD (or BIZARRE . . . or ABNORMAL) as you want!

🔍 DETECTIVE'S NOTEBOOK: THE DETECTIVE

The problem with having secrets is that sooner or later, you tend to run into someone who wants to find out what they are.

In a mystery story, that someone is the **detective**

character. A detective can be *anyone*. There are mysteries where the detective is a kid, a police officer, a grandmother, a dog, a robot, a magical talking doughnut machine—the possibilities are endless. As long as they're trying to dig up secrets and solve a mystery, they're a detective.

Usually, the detective is the **main character** of the story—and you may have guessed by now that in *Digging Up Danger*, Eliza is our detective. Since the reader is going to be spending a lot of time with the detective, it's important to think about this character in detail, so you know them inside and out. One way to do that is by writing out your ideas in an organizer, like our Detective Dossier on page 211.

On the dossier, there are a bunch of questions to get you thinking about the detective character. Let's take a look at each one!

Who is your detective?

What's their name? Are they a kid? An FBI agent? A vampire? A talking piece of cheese?

Why are they solving the mystery?

There are two main possibilities:

1. *They were hired.* In this case, it's the character's *job* to be a detective. For example:
   - They might work for the police, or the FBI, or a secret agency from your imagination, and are

☠ DETECTIVE DOSSIER ☠

Who is your detective?

Eliza Stahl, a teenage girl

Why are they solving the mystery? (Were they HIRED or is the mystery PERSONAL?)

It's <u>personal</u>. She wants to find the ghost in the plant store where she's spending the summer.

What else do they like to do (besides solving mysteries)?

Hunt for ghosts
Read books

What FEARS or WEAK-NESSES do they have?

Change. She likes things to <u>stay the same</u>.

What SKILLS make them a good detective?

Powers of observation: she's very good at noticing tiny clues, like sounds, changes in temperature, details of how people look.

Curiosity: she's very, very curious, and won't stop investigating

What else should the reader know about this character? Write your answer, or draw a picture!

She stretches when she gets nervous

Stretching fingers

Stretching tongue

Ghost-hunting equipment

Stack of books

She loves spooky stories

always on the lookout for mysteries that need solving.

- They might be a private investigator. That means they don't work for the police, but people pay them for their help solving mysteries. Private investigators are very popular in mystery stories, because it can be a lot of fun to make your detective a total weirdo who would never fit in working for the police, but who solves cases in their own strange way.

- Or maybe your character isn't *exactly* a detective, but is still getting paid to solve a mystery. For example: a scientist hired to figure out what's happening with a mysterious plant, a reporter hired to write a news report about a mystery, or a professional treasure hunter hired to find lost pirate gold.

OR

2. *It's personal.* For Eliza, the mystery is **personal.** In this case, the detective isn't getting paid to solve a mystery; they're solving it because they *want* to. Here are some more examples:
    - Maybe something weird is happening in the setting (like the plant store where they're spending the summer, or the school where they go every

day, or the spooky castle down the street from their home) and they decide to investigate.

- Maybe something important to *them* goes missing, and they decide to find it themselves. It can make for a very exciting story if your detective is searching for their own missing diary ... or missing treasure ... or missing ray gun with mysterious powers that they'd been hiding under the bed.

- Your character could just be really nosy, and decides to solve a mystery that has nothing to do with them, even though everyone keeps telling them to mind their own business. Some folks just can't *stand* it when people are hiding secrets, and will keep digging around no matter what, until they figure out what's going on.

What else do they like to do (besides solving mysteries)?

Detectives don't spend every hour of every day solving mysteries. Learning about what they do in their spare time can make them more believable, interesting characters. They might enjoy chess, or playing the violin, or walking their dog, or challenging their little brother at video games. There isn't really a wrong answer, as long as *you* think it would be an interesting choice. Sometimes the thing they like to do will also wind up helping them solve the mystery. For example, Eliza spends her spare time ghost hunting, and as you keep reading, you'll see that the skills she's picked up while doing that come in handy.

What fears or weaknesses do they have?

Giving a character a weakness is very important in any story, and is *definitely* important for a detective. If the detective has no weaknesses, solving the mystery will be too easy, and the story won't be very exciting! Think carefully about your detective's weakness as you work on your story. If they're afraid of frogs, will the mystery involve a missing frog? If they don't know how to swim, will they wind up looking for clues on a boat? For Eliza, her main weakness is that she doesn't like new places—or change of any kind. This is going to make solving the case extra challenging for her, since she's going to be in a place that makes her nervous and uncomfortable the whole time. (Plus, she's just a kid, and as you'll see soon, she's about to stumble into some serious, adult problems. . . .)

What skills make them a good detective?

How does your detective go about solving a case? What are some of their strengths that make them the right person for the job? Again, there are no wrong answers to this, but here are some popular choices:

- *Powers of observation.* Is your character someone who notices tiny details and can see clues where nobody else thinks to look for them? Eliza is good at this kind of thing: She has a lot of practice listening for far-off sounds, or noticing faint movements or changes of temperature, because she's always on the lookout for ghosts.

- *Puzzle solver.* Just finding clues isn't enough, of course. You also have to be able to figure out what they *mean.* Some stories about private detectives start when a police officer walks in with a bunch of clues and says, "I need your help! I can't figure out what all this means!" A very good puzzle solver can help make sense of even the weirdest clues that nobody else knows what to do with.

- *Master of disguise.* Some detectives are good at putting on disguises and pretending to be someone else. If the mystery takes place in a grocery store, for example, the detective might have a better chance of finding clues if they dress up like someone who works there. Or maybe they have a secret plan to get inside a mysterious mansion by pretending to be a plumber, there to fix the pipes.

- *People person.* Some detectives are just really good at talking to people. They get people to like them and convince them to share important clues . . . or make people afraid of them, and scare them into sharing important clues ... or trick people into giving away clues by asking just the right questions.

- *Uncontrollable curiosity.* Sometimes the most important thing for a detective is that they just really, *really* want to find out about secrets. This can lead them to take big risks, travel to dangerous places, sneak around where they might be discovered, and go on secret missions that leave the reader on the edge of their seat, almost saying out loud, "Don't do it! You don't know what's behind that door! It could be anything!" (As you'll see, this also describes Eliza extremely well.)

What else should the reader know about this character?

This is for any other details that you think are interesting or important. What does the detective look like? Draw it! What is their personality like? Write a little bit about it! Do they have any weird habits/clothing items/friends/anything else you want the reader to know? In Eliza's case, whenever she's nervous she takes a break to stretch!

⚡ IDEA STORM: CREATE A DETECTIVE

Create a detective for your own mystery! Decide if they're **hired** to solve the mystery or if the case is **personal.** Then decide what kind of character they are, what kind of **skills** they have that make them a good detective, and all the other interesting details that will bring them to life for the reader. If you want to use a Detective Dossier like we used for Eliza on page 211, draw your own and get started!

Don't forget that you definitely have PERMISSION TO GET WEIRD. Some of the greatest detectives in the history of mystery writing are *extremely* weird people. That makes them all the more fun to read about.

One final important note: A while back, we said that in the **beginning** of the mystery story, a mystery is discovered, and a character decides to solve it. Now we know that Eliza has decided to solve the mystery in *Digging Up Danger,* so congratulations! We are almost to the **middle** of the story! Buckle up, because this is where things get really wild. There's just one more piece of unfinished business to deal with first. . . .

Before we get to the **middle** of the story, there's one last secret to decide on. It's probably the most important secret in the whole mystery: *whodunit?*

Sometimes mystery stories are actually called "whodunits." As in: Who "done" it? Who caused the mystery?

The character who "done it" is called the **culprit.** In many stories, this character is a criminal: They stole the diamonds, or committed the murder. But they don't *have* to be a criminal, and sometimes it can make for a more interesting or surprising story if they have unusual reasons for causing the mystery. Maybe all the water is missing from the pool . . . because the culprit was searching for buried treasure under the pool, and the water came out when they dug through the bottom. Maybe the tiger is in the restaurant . . . because the culprit is training tigers to be guards at her mansion, and this one got away!

The reader should have no idea who the culprit is until the **end** of the mystery. It's usually *the biggest secret* the writer is hiding. You want to keep the reader guessing for the whole story about who the culprit is, as you drop little hints here and there along the way. If you do this well, when your reader finally gets to the end, they should look back at the whole story and see that it fits together like pieces in a puzzle, and suddenly all the weird things that happened will make sense. Which is why, once again, you need to decide on the **end** of the story while you're still writing the **beginning**.

To create a culprit, it can help to write out your ideas on an organizer, like our Culprit Case File. Take a look at one we put together for the culprit in *Digging Up Danger* on the next page.

CULPRIT CASE FILE

Who is your culprit?

What did the culprit do to cause the mystery? How did it happen?

Why did they do it?

What will happen if someone finds out this person is the culprit?

Draw the culprit! Label any important details about what they look like.

NOW COME UP WITH A RIDICULOUS NUMBER OF DETAILS ABOUT THE CULPRIT!
(THIS WILL HELP YOU MAKE UP CLUES LATER.)

Where does the culprit work? (Or if they don't work, where do they spend most of the day?)

What do they like to do in their spare time?

What do they like to eat?

What kind of music do they like?

What friends or family are important to them?

Where do they live?

What do they usually wear?

What objects do they usually carry around with them?

What kind of transportation do they usually use (car, train, helicopter)?

Where were they born?

What does their voice sound like?

What's another important detail about them?

Hey! Why is that thing blank?

You didn't think we were going to give away the culprit *that* easily, did you? Like we already said, it's *the biggest secret* in the book! It says TOP SECRET right there on the Case File! The culprit in *Digging Up Danger* is going to have to remain a secret for now—the same way you're going to be keeping the culprit a secret from your readers in your own mystery story.

Let's look more closely at the Culprit Case File, and talk about how to make your own culprit.

Who is your culprit?

What's their name? Are they human/animal/other? Are they a character we meet right away in the story, who is secretly the culprit the whole time? Or are they an outsider who came into the setting and caused the mystery?

What did the culprit do to cause the mystery? How did it happen?

This is very important. Get as specific as you can about *what* the culprit did and *how* it happened. When your detective is trying to solve the case, figuring out *how* the mystery happened is sometimes just as important as figuring out "whodunit."

Why did they do it?

Did they want to get rich? Was the mystery a way to

hide an even bigger secret? (If there's no Ferris wheel to ride, nobody will be up high enough to see what's hidden on the roof, down the street.) Maybe it was an accident. (They didn't mean for the tiger to get loose in that restaurant.) Or is the reason much weirder? (Their spaceship ran out of fuel, so they had to land it in the park. They've been in hiding ever since.)

What will happen if someone finds out this person is the culprit?

Usually the culprit doesn't want to get caught—that's part of why it's a mystery! They're afraid of what might happen if anyone finds out they did it. Think carefully about why your culprit might want to keep things a secret. (Here's a *bonus* challenge for you: The most common answer to this question is that they'll go to jail. But that's been done *a lot*, so you will make things more interesting if you can think of a totally different reason they might not want someone to find out.)

What about the details?

Finally, there's a whole other sheet to plan out a RIDIC-ULOUS number of details about the culprit. Why should you ask yourself all these little questions? This is all about helping you come up with **clues** for the detective to find. Stay tuned for more on that very soon.

⚡ IDEA STORM: CREATE A CULPRIT

Now you try it! Use the Culprit Case File from page 220 as a guide and create a **culprit** of your own. Think carefully about what they did to cause the mystery, and *why* they decided to do it. Then think up as many details as you possibly can about this character. Seriously, TONS and TONS of details. So many details it's almost RIDICULOUS. This will give you a lot of choices when you're making up **clues** later to help your detective.

Be sure to remember the culprit is usually a HUGE secret from the readers. After you make the Culprit Case File, you might even want to fold it in half and write the words TOP SECRET on the back, just to remind yourself how big this secret is. Even if the readers meet the character early in the story (in some mysteries, the readers meet the culprit right on the first page), *they shouldn't find out that this character is the culprit* until the **end** of the story.

We probably don't even need to tell you by now, but you have PERMISSION TO GET WEIRD when you're making up this culprit. Let your imagination run wild!

THE MIDDLE:
THE INVESTIGATION

🔍 DETECTIVE'S NOTEBOOK:
THE INVESTIGATION (KEEPING TRACK OF CLUES)

We've arrived at the **middle** of our mystery story! The middle is all about the **investigation,** when the detective will be looking for **clues** to solve the mystery.

What is a clue?

A clue is basically a *hint* about your mystery. The detective will need to find lots of these hints before being able to solve the case—and your readers will be very interested to see these hints as well, to try to figure out the secret for themselves.

Eliza is a natural detective, so she's already started trying to keep track of the clues in her ghost notebook (even though she hasn't found any really important clues . . . yet):

> *June 10. ES (Eliza Stahl). Potential ghost sighting: dark figure in front of shop. Approx. 2:00 p.m.*

> *June 10. ES. Potential ghost activity (creaking sound): attic. Approx. 2:30 p.m.*

How do you put clues into your own mystery?

This is a big reason why the writer needs to know who the culprit is while they're still writing the **beginning** of their story. In order for your detective to find a clue, *you* have to know all about the culprit, so you can pick a clue that makes sense! Go back to your Culprit Case File and look at the RIDICULOUS number of details you planned out. What is something about your culprit you'd like to turn into a clue? Do they have huge shoes, and leave a trail of huge footprints wherever they go? Do they love pizza, and the detective finds a long string of cheese across the floor? Do they wear a yellow coat, and someone saw a person in a yellow coat near the mystery? There's no wrong answer, you just need to think about a clue that's right for *your* culprit.

When you're coming up with clues, it's also a good time to think about the *five senses* again. For example, in *Digging Up Danger*, Eliza is very tuned in to using her senses to search for clues. She keeps a lookout for shadows (or shadowy figures), listens carefully for sounds (like the creaking in the attic), and is always trying to feel for changes in temperature, which might indicate a ghost. If *your* culprit is sneaking around somewhere in the setting, does the detective see or hear anything? Is there a certain kind of sound, smell, or even taste that could be a clue about your culprit. ("Why does this salad taste like butterscotch? It's almost as though someone who works in a butterscotch factory was leaning over it and accidentally dripped butterscotch on it. . . .")

While you're working on your mystery, it can help to plan ahead and think about the clues you are going to want the detective to find. You can use an Investigation Record, like the one on page 228, to organize your thoughts.

Eliza's investigation has barely begun, so we won't give away any of the big clues she's about to dig up! But later on, we'll look at a completed Investigation Record, so you can see how Eliza's whole investigation looks.

So far, Eliza didn't have to try very hard to find clues. She was just observant as she went about her daily life, and the clues landed right in front of her. But as the mystery goes on, she's going to have to work harder and put herself in more danger to find the clues she really needs to solve the case. Get ready—this story is about to get taken up a notch. . . .

📝 MYSTERY WRITER CHALLENGE: THE RIGHT CLUES FOR YOU

If you've filled out a Culprit Case File, then you've already started thinking about clues, but choosing *just the right clues* is important for a mystery writer. Let's get in a little bit of practice looking at clues and trying to guess what they're hinting at, in a game we call "Who Left the Clues?" Turn to page 229 to play.

☠ INVESTIGATION RECORD ☠

Clue	How did the Detective find the clue?

Clue	How did the Detective find the clue?

Clue	How did the Detective find the clue?

Clue	How did the Detective find the clue?

Clue	How did the Detective find the clue?

Clue	How did the Detective find the clue?

You don't have to fill out the whole thing—but you also don't have to stop there! If there are more clues, keep the record going on another page!

Below are some clues from a few different cases. Take a look at each, and see if you can figure out *what kind of culprit* they're giving you hints about.

1.

- When I tried to smell the flower, it squirted water in my face.
- The footprints were huge—at least two feet long.
- The footprints stopped in front of a brightly colored tent. There was a round red fake nose on the ground.

Too easy? Here's one that's slightly harder:

2.

- Around the time the candy disappeared, the cashier saw someone with an extremely shiny smile.
- Something was stuck to my shoe. It looked like a long piece of string, but it smelled minty.
- Through the wall, I could hear the sound of a very tiny drill.

Did you get it? Here's an even harder one:

3.

- The floor was scuffed up with tread marks from a tire.

- The refrigerator was on top of the car. Who would have been strong enough to lift that?
- The note simply read: "01101000 01101001."

The answers are on page 275.

Try this out for yourself! Before you write a whole story, imagine a few different culprits and come up with clues about them. Try out the clues on your friends and family to see if they can guess the answer. This will be good practice for when you put clues in your own mystery.

 IDEA STORM: PLAN THE INVESTIGATION

Draw up your own version of the Investigation Record, and start planning what **clues** you want your detective to find. The best place to start getting ideas for clues is the Culprit Case File (see pages 220–221). Look at the RIDICULOUS number of details to help you decide what kind of clues *your* culprit would leave behind.

How does the detective find all these clues? The clues are probably not all just sitting together on a table, waiting for the detective to find them, after all. As you keep reading, we're going to give you lots of ideas for how a detective tracks down the clues they need, and you'll end up with many options to choose from. For now, just think about the clues themselves, and write down the ones you want your detective to find. We'll help you with the rest as we keep going.

🔍 DETECTIVE'S NOTEBOOK: SNOOPING AROUND

There are lots of different ways for a detective to look for clues, but let's start with a simple, old-fashioned one: snooping around.

This is the easiest thing for a detective to do, really. Is there a part of the setting they haven't visited yet? Maybe there's a place they've been told not to go, or a place that is supposed to be private. If the setting is an amusement park, does the detective try to look around in the Ferris wheel control booth? If the story takes place in a school, does a kid detective sneak into the teacher's lounge when nobody is looking?

In Eliza's case, she thinks there's something weird going on in the basement and wants to find out more. She already went down there once, during the day, but she got caught. (That happens to detectives a lot when they're snooping around!) So now she's headed back at night, when she thinks everyone will be safely asleep.

If you just read Chapter 8, you know what happened

next. Let's point out two very important things that Eliza found:

1. *An unexpected secret.* Eliza was going down in the basement to look for ghosts, but instead she found . . . plants. Secret plants. *Dangerous* plants. What is Mr. Carroll up to? When you go snooping around, you don't always find what you expect to find. Sometimes you dig up a new secret you didn't even suspect was there (even if the *writer* had a secret planned for their setting all along). This secret doesn't even have to be a clue in the mystery . . . though in Eliza's case, it probably is.
2. *A clue about the culprit.* Besides discovering what was in the basement, Eliza found another clue: the ghost, or whatever it is that's haunting this store, has "a pair of blazing yellow eyes." Eliza's snooping around paid off! She found a new clue that may turn out to be very important.

Also, the moment when Eliza saw the yellow eyes was another great example of keeping the reader in **suspense.** Go back and read Chapter 8 one more time. Notice how slowly and mysteriously we learned about what Eliza saw. Any time your detective finds a shocking clue, it's a great excuse to take things slowly and keep your reader in suspense.

IDEA STORM: MAKE THE DETECTIVE SNOOP AROUND

Would you like your detective to do some snooping around? It's easy to do: Just think about a place in your setting where the detective hasn't been yet, or isn't supposed to go, and have them look there. You might also want to go back to the Detective Dossier (see page 211), and think about how your detective would use their **skills** to snoop around. For example, if they're a master of disguise, do they put on a costume and pretend to be someone else to get where they want to go? Or if they have great powers of observation, it's possible they don't need to snoop for very long. Maybe all they need is for someone to open a door for them so they can look around for five seconds to see if they notice any clues.

What will your detective find while snooping around? That's up to you, but here are a few ideas to get you started:

1. *An unexpected secret.* Eliza found dangerous plants, but the secret in *your* story could be anything: Maybe your detective spoils the preparation for a surprise party . . . or finds an animal they didn't know was there . . . or an escaped convict . . . or a secret laboratory. It can be a big secret, a small secret, or *maybe even the secret about your setting* from way back on the Mystery Setting organizer!

2. *A clue about the culprit.* You should have already read "Detective's Notebook: The Investigation (Keeping Track of Clues)" on page 225, and started to fill out your own Investigation Record (if you didn't, go do that now!). While your detective is snooping around, it's a great time for them to find one of the clues you've been planning that gives a hint about who your culprit is. Look at your Investigation Record, under "How did the detective find this clue?" and write down where and how the detective was snooping around. For example: "Eliza was snooping around the house at night."

3. *They get caught.* This happens a lot in mysteries! Before they're able to see any clues, or uncover any secrets, somebody catches the detective in the act of snooping around. They'll have to try again later. This can also be a great way to create **suspense.** If the detective gets caught before they can look inside the basement (or the teachers' lounge . . . or the Ferris wheel control booth . . . or wherever you decide to send them), then your reader will be wondering, "What's in there?" They'll suspect there's some kind of secret and will be excited for the detective to finally go back there later.

🔍 DETECTIVE'S NOTEBOOK:
WATCH OUT FOR SUSPICIOUS BEHAVIOR

What in the world was Tommy up to? Why did he act so nervous when the "ghost" left the shop? Where did he really go when he said he was headed out for a walk? Why did he sneak into the room with the rare plants? What happened to his *eyes*? What could explain this **suspicious behavior**?

Suspicious behavior is a great clue to put in a mystery story. If someone is acting strangely, and doing things that don't seem to make sense, or that are very secretive, that could be a sign that they're up to no good or have something to hide.

How does a detective spot suspicious behavior? Sometimes it's similar to what Eliza did: They **follow** someone to see where they're going, and notice suspicious behavior along the way. In some cases a detective might go on a **stakeout:** they hide in one spot where they think the culprit might show up, and watch to see if anything suspicious happens. Or sometimes a **witness** tells the detective about the suspicious behavior. A witness is a character who sees something important about the mystery. ("I saw a pizza delivery truck parked by the amusement park, and the delivery guy was climbing the fence. Don't you think that sounds suspicious, Detective?")

Does this suspicious behavior mean Tommy is the culprit? Not necessarily. What he did was *definitely* strange, but there might be a reason for his behavior we don't know yet.

Since we can't tell you more yet about why Tommy did what he did, let's look at a few more examples of suspicious behavior to help you practice your skills.

📓 MYSTERY WRITER CHALLENGE: STUDYING SUSPICIOUS BEHAVIOR

Try this game called "Very Suspicious!"

It's midnight in the park. You're a detective on a stake-out. It's been quiet all evening, and you're starting to get sleepy. Suddenly, from behind a tree, you see something moving. A figure walks slowly into a nearby field, but it's too dark to see their face. They are holding something. . . . The light of the moon reflects off metal, and you realize that it's a shovel. The figure begins to dig in the field. And dig . . . and dig . . .

Why is this shadowy figure acting so suspiciously?

A. They are digging a hole to hide stolen jewels.

B. They stole some jewels many years ago and hid them in this field. Now they have finally returned to find them.

C. There is a top secret laboratory hidden under the park. They are trying to dig down to an entrance.

D. They work for the park and are planting flowers.

They work at night so they don't bother people during the day.

The answer is . . .

Keep reading for spoilers . . .

It could be any of these! That's the thing about suspicious behavior: It's *weird;* it makes you *suspect* that someone is up to no good. They *could* just be planting flowers (or something else totally innocent), but you can't say for sure quite yet. The detective needs to keep investigating.

Here are a couple more examples. For each one, see if you can come up with your own answer for option D that is completely different from the other possibilities.

1. It's a busy night at the restaurant. People are eating at every table, and waiters bring food back and forth from the kitchen. A woman is sneaking slowly through the restaurant: hiding behind curtains, ducking under tables, pretending to sit at a table for a moment, then crouching behind a chair, looking around.

Why is this woman acting so suspiciously?

A. She's the chef, and is spying on the customers to see how they like the food.

237

B. She's a detective, and is doing a terrible job snooping around to look for clues.

C. She used to be a cat, but has been transformed into a human. She's just acting normal—for a cat.

D. *What other reason can you come up with for her suspicious behavior?*

2. The winter has been cold, and there is snow piled up behind the old castle. A window opens high in a tower, and a kid appears, quickly throws a big red bag out the window, then shuts the window and is gone again. The bag falls down and sinks out of sight under the snow.

Why was this kid acting so suspiciously?

A. The bag is full of candy the kid has been secretly hiding. He threw it out the window to get rid of the evidence.

B. There's a small but very dangerous animal in the bag. The kid caught it in the castle, then got it outside as quickly as possible.

C. The kid was supposed to take the garbage out but was being *suuuuper* lazy.

D. *What other reason can you come up with for his suspicious behavior?*

⚡ IDEA STORM: MAKE A CHARACTER DO SOMETHING SUSPICIOUS

Think about your setting and then think about something a character could do there that would be unusual . . . weird . . . **suspicious.** Decide why *you* think the character is being suspicious. Are they protecting a *secret* somewhere in the setting? Are they the culprit, and the suspicious behavior winds up being an important clue? Are they doing something innocent that just *looks* suspicious? Or is the answer something weirder?

Be sure to decide how the detective sees the suspicious behavior. Are they **following** the character? Are they on a **stakeout**? Do they hear about it from a **witness**?

If the suspicious behavior ends up providing a **clue** (Tommy was in the rare plant room, and has *yellow eyes*), you can make a note of it in your Investigation Record (see page 228). And at the very least, maybe the person acting suspicious will turn out to be a suspect. . . .

🔍 DETECTIVE'S NOTEBOOK: IDENTIFY THE SUSPECTS

"Which one of them did it?"

That's what you want your reader wondering. Don't make it too easy for them, either. If there's only one other person in the story besides the detective, it's going to be pretty obvious who the culprit is. For that reason, you need to give your readers plenty of **suspects** to choose from: other characters who *might* have done it.

If you want to decide on some suspects, the easiest place to start is with your setting. Remember when we asked you to pick a setting with lots of people around? This is why! Ask yourself: Who spends time in the setting? What **motive** (or reason) would they have for causing the mystery? If they have a good motive, they might be the culprit.

In Chapter 11, we met a new suspect who might be behind Eliza's ghost mystery . . . and found out some disturbing new details about other characters who could be suspects, too. What motives do they have? What is the evidence against them? Take a look on page 241.

We can't say for sure yet who the culprit is . . . but this list of suspects gives us a place to start! The detective needs to look more closely at all of these suspects to see what else we can find out. How does the detective do that? As we discussed in "Detective's Notebook: Watch Out for Suspicious Behavior," they might **follow** them, or go on a **stakeout.** They might **snoop around** near where the suspect spends time. They might also just ask the suspect a lot of **questions** about the mystery to see what they can find out. For one example of that, read the next chapter!

SUSPECT #1: MR. CARROLL

MOTIVE: He's dealing in dangerous plants. Maybe trying to scare Eliza away from his secrets.

EVIDENCE AGAINST HIM: Eliza saw him bringing plants in through the basement.

OTHER DETAILS: Makes horrible puns all the time

SUSPECT #2: MRS. CARROLL

MOTIVE: Works with her husband, may be helping him

EVIDENCE AGAINST HER: Nothing conclusive

OTHER DETAILS: Talks to plants

SUSPECT #3: TOMMY

MOTIVE: Could be trying to protect his uncle

EVIDENCE AGAINST HIM: Suspicious behavior, yellow eyes

OTHER DETAILS: Very interested in plants; very shy and weird around Eliza

SUSPECT #4: WEIRD CUSTOMER

MOTIVE: Being a ghost (?)

EVIDENCE AGAINST HIM: Old-timey way of talking. Moves silently. Could be a ghost!!

OTHER DETAILS: Wide hat, long coat, sunglasses, Moggie growled at him

SUSPECT #5: MOGGIE

MOTIVE: Unknown

EVIDENCE AGAINST HER: Yellow eyes

OTHER DETAILS: A dog, so probably not the top suspect

SUSPECT #6: UNKNOWN

Who was that guy handing plants to Mr. Carroll in the basement? Is there anyone else hanging around that we don't know about?

🌩️ IDEA STORM: CREATE SOME SUSPECTS

Come up with some suspects of your own! You can draw pictures of them and keep track of what their motives might be, what the evidence is against them, and any other details you want to remember.

Here's another important thing detectives often look for with their suspects: an **alibi.** If the suspect has an alibi, that means they were somewhere else when the mystery took place, so they probably couldn't be the culprit. If the suspect doesn't have an alibi (or if the alibi turns out to be a lie), the detective will have reason to be very suspicious.

If your detective **follows** a suspect, or goes on a **stakeout,** asks the suspect **questions, snoops around,** and ends up finding **clues,** be sure to note that on your Investigation Record (see page 228).

🔍 DETECTIVE'S NOTEBOOK: THE CULPRIT STRIKES AGAIN!

It's every detective's worst fear: Yet another thing is MISSING ("First the diamonds were stolen from the museum, now a priceless painting!") or something new is

WEIRD or DOESN'T BELONG in the setting ("The murderer has struck again!").

Sometimes, though, this actually *helps* the detective to get important new clues that help solve the case. Causing a mystery is risky, and every time the culprit does it, there's more and more chance of getting caught.

For example, when the rare plant went MISSING, Eliza thought Tommy might have had something to do with it. That's what made her decide to **question** Mr. and Mrs. Carroll, which is when she found her next clue: They both had *yellow eyes*! Now she knows that no matter what is causing all these mysterious events, the Carrolls must be involved somehow, which will be very important when she decides what to do next. . . .

IDEA STORM: WILL YOUR CULPRIT STRIKE AGAIN?

Do you want the culprit to strike again in your mystery? You don't have to—not all mysteries do this. But if you do, here's how you might think about it:

Decide *why* the culprit did it. Was it the same reason they did it the first time? If they dug a hole in the bottom of the pool looking for treasure . . . do they dig a hole in the bottom of *another* pool, looking for treasure again? Or maybe they were trying to get rid of evidence—was there an important clue inside the pizza dough, so they ate it before anyone could find it?

Decide *how* they did it. Did anyone see the culprit do something suspicious? Did they leave any new clues behind? Once again, you can look at your Culprit Case File on pages 220–221 to get ideas for what kind of clues they might end up leaving. If they always wear lots of necklaces, does someone hear the sound of jangling jewelry near where the mystery happens? If they work at a pancake factory, does a smell of pancakes linger in the air?

🔍 DETECTIVE'S NOTEBOOK: FOLLOWING A LEAD

Eliza finally gets a chance in Chapter 13 to follow a **lead** she's been wanting to tackle since much earlier in the book: She and her mom are headed to the attic.

A lead is a kind of clue—but it's a clue that "leads" the detective to *go somewhere* or *talk to someone new*. For example, Eliza has had several leads that have pointed her toward the attic. Not only has she heard strange sounds coming from there, but the attic key has been hidden for many chapters, causing her to think someone is trying to keep her out. With some assistance from her mom, who

244

is now helping her investigate, she has a chance to finally follow up on those leads.

If you've read Chapter 13, you already know what happens next, but let's take a moment to point out two important things she finds:

1. *Another clue.* Whoever the culprit is, there are clues that they were indeed up in the attic. There's a leaf from the missing plant, so whoever took it must have had it locked up there at some point.
2. *An unexpected obstacle.* Someone locks the door while they're inside! More about this in the next chapter.

Following up on a lead can be a great way to move the story forward. It gives your detective a new place to **snoop around,** or a new person to ask **questions** of, and it may even put them in danger, causing some unexpected excitement. . . .

MYSTERY WRITER CHALLENGE: WHERE WILL THE CLUES LEAD?

Sometimes **leads** are really obvious. If the detective hears a noise in the attic, it makes sense they might want to look in the attic. Or if the detective hears someone say "I wonder where Mrs. Sandwich is? I haven't seen her since the mystery started," then the detective is probably going to want to go find Mrs. Sandwich and ask her questions.

But sometimes leads are trickier than that, and the detective has to do a little bit of puzzle solving to figure out what they mean. Here's a game called "Follow the Lead." Decide where each lead is telling you to go!

1. Racing out of the amusement park went a little red car. If you looked very closely, you could just make out the model of a pizza on its roof as it sped away.

Where should the detective follow that car? Too easy? Here's a trickier one:

2. In her sleep, she shouted out "barking, so many different barks, yips, woofs, howls, high and low."

The answers are on page 275.

Sometimes the detective finds another kind of lead, one that turns into a mini-mystery all its own, such as a note, a riddle, or a code they can't figure out right away. For example:

"The note read *'I hid it where the stairs meet the rushing water, by the bony hand.'*"

What does that mean? Are there stairs near some water in the setting? Or is it a code? Are there rocks that *look* like stairs going down to a river? And what's the bony hand? Part of a skeleton? A tree that looks like a bony hand? The answer will be up to the writer's imagination! The detective is just going to have to ask people what it means, or walk around the setting looking for a place that could fit the riddle, until they finally realize, "Bony hand? Why, that broken-down old building looks just like a bony hand!"

This can be fun to try yourself. Practice writing out a riddle like this at home and see if anyone can guess what you mean. Maybe there's a table with four thick legs that reminds you of an animal, and the couch nearby is dark black. You might say "Between the wooden four-legged beast, and the fluffy rock dark as midnight, this is where the remote control lies." Or you can just draw a treasure map!

IDEA STORM: LEAD YOUR DETECTIVE TO THE CLUE

Try putting a **lead** in your story: a clue that tells the detective *where* to go, or *whom* to question next. The lead might be really simple, like a noise, a smell, or another big clue from the five senses that points the way. Someone could even just *tell* the detective the clue.

Or the lead might be a bit trickier, like a riddle, a note, or even a treasure map. The detective has to figure out what it really means.

Once the detective follows up on the lead, you can decide what happens next:

1. *Do they find another clue?* If so, go back to your Investigation Record (on page 228) to make a note of how they find it.
2. *Is there an unexpected obstacle?* This can make things very exciting. Keep reading to find out more about it.

DETECTIVE'S NOTEBOOK: RUNNING INTO AN UNEXPECTED OBSTACLE

Now things are really heating up. While Eliza and her mom were investigating the attic, they got locked in! They might be in danger!

Sometimes the culprit throws in an unexpected **obstacle** (something to try to stop the detective from finishing their investigation) so they never find out the real secret behind the

DANGER!

mystery. The obstacle could be anything, but it's usually something that puts the detective in *danger*. For example, the main characters could be locked in a room, or have their equipment tampered with (they're driving in a car when suddenly the brakes don't work, or they're in outer space when their oxygen supply starts leaking), or be attacked in some way (a vicious dog approaches them, or a snake appears in their room, or a robot goes haywire and tries to crush them), or anything else that makes them afraid to keep investigating.

How does the detective get past the obstacle? The answer is up to you, but it's usually the most exciting if they try a few different things before finally getting to a solution that works. For example, check out the "Get Past the Obstacle Organizer" we filled out for Eliza and her mom on page 250.

Eliza's mom starts off with a logical solution to just call the police. Unfortunately, of course, the phone has been left downstairs.

Then they have to start getting more creative and think about crawling out the window. But they decide it's too dangerous. Maybe if they were locked in for days with no food or water, or if they were being attacked, they might risk it. For now, they move on to option three. . . .

Eliza's mom, who is a botanist and knows a lot about how chemicals work, finds a way to literally blow the door off its hinges. They run out, only to find something even more unexpected when they make it downstairs. . . .

☠ GET PAST THE OBSTACLE ☠

WHAT IS THE OBSTACLE?
Eliza and her mom are locked in the attic!

THE **FIRST** SOLUTION MY CHARACTER TRIED:

Call the police

UNFORTUNATELY . . . (WHAT WENT WRONG?):

They left the phone downstairs.

THE **NEXT** THING MY CHARACTER TRIED:

Climb out the window

UNFORTUNATELY . . . (WHAT WENT WRONG?):

It's too dangerous:
they might fall,
and it's four stories high.

THE SOLUTION THAT **FINALLY** WORKED:

Use a chemical reaction to blast the door open.

IT WORKED BECAUSE:

Eliza's mom is a scientist who knows how to do it—and has a fire extinguisher handy.

 **IDEA STORM: THROW DOWN AN OBSTACLE**

Try putting an unexpected **obstacle** in your story! Decide on something that puts the detective in *danger*, and makes them afraid to continue the investigation. Then decide how they get past the obstacle. If the first couple of ways they try to get past the obstacle don't work, that's great! It makes the obstacle seem even worse, and makes your story even more exciting.

You might think about your detective's *skills* (as outlined in the Detective Dossier on page 211), and how that helps them find a solution. Eliza's mom uses her knowledge of science to get them out of danger, but your detective might overcome obstacles in a very different way. For example:

- Are they very *observant*, and notice an important detail that helps them get past the obstacle? ("That panel on the wall looks different from all the others. If I press on it, will I find a way to exit the room?")
- Are they a *puzzle solver*, who figures out an extremely creative way out of trouble? ("I'm being attacked by a snake and a tiger at the same time . . . but what if I can get them angry at each other instead of at me?")
- Do they have a *disguise* that helps them? ("If I can just make it into the basketball stadium, I can

MYSTERY CREATION ZONE

dress up like one of the players and escape the guy who's chasing me.")

- Are they a *people person*, and talk their way out? ("You don't want to hurt me with that flaming bow and arrow. I know you're a better person than that. Plus, I think we could help each other out.")

There's no wrong answer to this. Just think about the obstacle *you* came up with, and decide how *your* detective would handle it. As always, you definitely have PERMISSION TO GET WEIRD!

MYSTERY WRITER CHALLENGE: PERMISSION TO GET WEIRD

In every mystery, you eventually get to the part where most of the characters transform into dogs. Practice this yourself in a game called "They're All Dogs Now." To begin, you . . .

Wait—WHAT? WHAT JUST HAPPENED?

This is just a reminder: Every mystery does NOT have to be about a criminal trying to do evil and then getting caught. Sometimes the answers turn out to be MUCH weirder than that. If Eliza had started out looking for ghosts, but it turned out she'd just been hearing a criminal

252

sneaking around . . . on the one hand, that would have made sense. It could even have been an exciting story! But it can also be a thrill for readers to have a mystery turn into something much stranger than they ever expected.

Don't be afraid to get very, very WEIRD!

🔍 DETECTIVE'S NOTEBOOK: QUESTIONING A WITNESS

Sooner or later, the detective is usually going to end up questioning a **witness.** A witness is someone who saw something important, and might know about some clues that could end up cracking the case. For example, Mr. Carroll's business associate Leif has *quite* the story to tell about where he first got the plant, and gives a surprising clue: Someone . . . or some*thing* . . . has been following him and the plant from the island where he first picked it up. Whoever . . . or *what*ever . . . it is must be the culprit with yellow eyes, who has been sneaking around the house, and who finally stole the plant.

There are two kinds of witnesses in a mystery story:

1. *Truthful witnesses.* These witnesses are telling the truth. You can safely believe everything they say, and use those clues to help solve the mystery. Is Leif a truthful witness? Well, his story is pretty weird, but it seems to fit the facts so far. It does seem like he's telling the truth (at least for the most part).

2. *Lying witnesses.* Sometimes witnesses are lying. Maybe they have something to hide. Maybe they're trying to protect someone else. Maybe they're not the culprit, but they don't want the detective to think they are, so they change the facts to make themselves sound better. Is Leif lying? It doesn't *seem* like it . . . but he's a strange character. He makes his living selling rare, dangerous, and possibly illegal plants, so he doesn't seem too trustworthy. And what's with his name: "Leif"? Is that pronounced like "Leaf"? Is that some kind of weird plant clue? Even if he's telling the truth, we'd better watch him closely.

📓 MYSTERY WRITER CHALLENGE: CATCHING A WITNESS IN A LIE

How can a detective tell if they have a **lying witness** on their hands? Sometimes the witness may say something that goes against the facts: They claim they've never visited the amusement park in their life, but then photographs turn up with them posing in front of the Ferris wheel! Sometimes, it's a little trickier. Sometimes the detective has to spot whether there's something suspicious about the story they're being told. Try it yourself in a game called "Why Is It a Lie?" See if you can spot what's suspicious about this story:

"It was 100 degrees that day, and I was on my way to the pool. I couldn't see well because I had my coat hood up and my heavy scarf wrapped around my face."

If it was 100 degrees, why would you wear a hood and scarf? Something about that story doesn't add up! The detective should be very suspicious!

Here are a couple more examples that are a little bit tougher. See if you can spot what's suspicious about these stories:

1. "It was the middle of the night when the power went out in the city. There was no moon, and the clouds even covered the stars. I was hurrying down the street to get home, because I didn't have

a flashlight and I was a little freaked out. That's when I looked toward the school about 100 feet away from me. Through the window, inside the principal's office, was a clown juggling dark blue beanbags!"

2. "This all started when I was a small child in 1979. I was going to a friend's birthday party, but I'd never been to her house before, so we got directions from the Internet. The directions turned out to be a little bit wrong, so we were late getting to the party. By the time I got there it had already happened: The whole house had disappeared!"

The answers are on page 275.

Try making one of these yourself! Write out a very short story, where a witness describes something that happened to them ... but put in one thing that doesn't make sense, and shows that they're probably lying. Show it to your friends and family, and see if they can guess what's suspicious! It will be great practice if you ever want to write about a lying witness in a mystery story.

IDEA STORM: WHO WILL BE A WITNESS?

Think about what kind of **witness** your detective will question. Is it someone from the setting, who was around when the mystery took place? Is it someone unexpected, who turns out to know some important clues about the mystery? Maybe the witness is a **suspect,** and the detective thinks they might be lying. If they are, that's an important clue as well!

Be sure to make a note of any important clues in your Investigation Record (see page 228). You definitely have PERMISSION to question a WEIRD witness!

DETECTIVE'S NOTEBOOK: STING OPERATION

In a **sting operation** the detective tricks the culprit into revealing themselves and proving they caused the mystery.

Eliza did this by letting the culprit know she had something he would want (the berries). Sometimes, a detective doesn't really have something the culprit would want, but they *trick* them, like in Eliza's mom's plan to put a computer up to the window with a picture of the plant.

How does a detective come up with an idea for a sting

operation? Sometimes they think about the mysteries the culprit has been causing, and try to lure them into **striking again** so they can be caught ("I'm replacing the stolen diamonds with some new, even more valuable diamonds. I SURE HOPE NOBODY TRIES TO STEAL THEM!").

Sometimes, the detective isn't sure who the culprit is, but they find a way to make the culprit *think* they do. For example, they go around saying "I found a witness who saw everything. I'm meeting them tomorrow night at seven." Then the next night at seven, the culprit shows up, because they want to know who this witness is.

Of course, once they've done a sting operation, the detective has a new problem to deal with: The culprit has been caught, and often the culprit doesn't want to stay caught. They might try to create some more **obstacles** that will put the detective in danger (as Eliza discovered).

But once a sting operation is over, the detective has usually solved the case! We are about to officially start the **end** of the story, where the mystery has been solved. Hooray!

 ## IDEA STORM: MOUNT A STING OPERATION

Not all mysteries have a **sting operation,** but if you want to put one in your mystery, think about how your detective could trick the culprit into revealing themselves. Do they have something the culprit wants (or do they find a way to make the culprit *think* they do)? Do they trick the culprit into trying to cause a new mystery, so they can catch them in the act? What happens when the culprit gets caught? Do they give up, or cause an **obstacle**? (For more obstacles, see the Obstacle Organizer on page 250.)

When you're thinking about a sting operation, you absolutely have PERMISSION TO GET WEIRD. Eliza's sting operation started out as a séance, where she tried to get a ghost to appear (and it ended up working, but not for the reason Eliza thought it would). Your detective's sting operation can be as weird as you want it to be.

🔍 DETECTIVE'S NOTEBOOK: WRAPPING UP THE INVESTIGATION (THE END IS JUST THE BEGINNING!)

Now that Eliza has wrapped up her investigation, let's take a look back at what she did to track down all those clues and find the culprit in the Investigation Record on page 260.

Eliza snooped around, spotted suspicious behavior, questioned suspects, followed a lead, and much more. Not every detective does every one of these things in every mystery, and they definitely don't have to be in the same order as Eliza did them. You might even come up with some totally different ways your detective finds clues! But by carefully choosing what clues you want ahead of time, and

Clue Mr. Carroll is getting secret, late-night plant deliveries in the basement	How did the Detective find the clue? Snooping around at night.
Clue Yellow <u>eyes</u> on a mysterious figure in the window!	How did the Detective find the clue? Snooping around at night.
Clue Tommy and the Carolls have <u>yellow eyes</u>!!	How did the Detective find the clue? Following Tommy, noticing his suspicious behavior Questioning the Carolls
Clue Gold leaves in the attic—someone was hiding the plant there	How did the Detective find the clue? Following a lead: Eliza heard noises coming from the attic
Clue Tommy and the Carolls can turn into dogs! That plant is <u>powerful</u>!	How did the Detective find the clue? Questioning Tommy and the Carolls
Clue Someone—or something—followed the plant all the way from a mysterious island. Time for a sting operation!	How did the Detective find the clue? Questioning a witness: Leif

You don't have to fill out the whole thing—but you also don't have to stop there! If there are more clues, keep the record going on another page!

MYSTERY CREATION ZONE

then planning out the whole investigation like this, you'll be in good shape to write a mystery that makes sense, with all the pieces fitting together.

However ... what if you're halfway through writing a mystery, and you suddenly get an idea for a more interesting mystery, or a different culprit, or a new kind of clue for the detective to discover? Can you go back and change your ideas?

Of course you can! That's the whole reason to skip lines, and be ready to cross things out, or hit the delete key. Sure, by the time your reader sees the story it looks neat and polished, but that's because you've kept the biggest secret of all from your readers the whole time: Writing a mystery takes very careful planning, and sometimes a lot of rewriting. It only looks easy to the reader because you work to *make* it look easy.

THE END: CRACKING THE CASE

🔍 DETECTIVE'S NOTEBOOK: CONFESSION AND CONSEQUENCES

We've arrived at the **end** of our mystery—not the very end, but close enough that we can now show you the Top Secret Culprit Case File for *Digging Up Danger* on page 263.

The dark figure Eliza saw hovering around the front of the plant store when she first arrived, the shadow she saw behind the greenhouse that she thought might have been "just a dog," the terrifying shape with the yellow eyes she saw through the window, all turned out to be William, Eliza's "ghost." But also, in a super weird twist, William's *plant* turned out to be the **co-culprit:** many of the weird things Eliza observed, from Tommy's suspicious behavior, to the Carrolls' yellow eyes, were actually caused by the plant!

When the culprit finally admits they're behind the mystery, this is called the **confession.** How does the detective get a culprit to confess? In our case, Eliza did a sting operation to lure the culprit out. Many detectives don't need a sting operation, however; they simply find enough clues to

MYSTERY CREATION ZONE

CULPRIT CASE FILE

Who is your culprit?

William the werewolf—and his <u>plant</u> that turns people into dogs

What did the culprit do to cause the mystery? How did it happen?

He prowled around Carolls' Gardens looking for his plant. Eliza thought he was a ghost. The plant's berries turned people into yellow-eyed dogs.

Why did they do it?

The plant was stolen from William's island, and he wants to get it back. And the plant turned people into yellow-eyed dogs because that's just what it does. It's a plant.

What will happen if someone finds out this person is the culprit?

William's home might be destroyed if people around the world go there looking for plants. And people everywhere might start turning into werewolves.

Draw the culprit! Label any important details about what they look like.

MYSTERY CREATION ZONE

263

prove the culprit did it, and tell everyone how they solved the mystery. The culprit has no choice but to confess.

The mystery writer's job is to make that confession as interesting as possible. After all, William didn't just say, "You caught me. I took the plant because it's from my island where dog people live. Good-bye forever!" He told an exciting *story* with his confession. Here are a few ideas for how the confession might go:

- *Make the culprit sympathetic.* The culprit doesn't have to be a bad guy. Sometimes they have good reasons for what they did, like William, trying to save his people from the outside world (and to save the outside world from his people). Even if the culprit isn't quite as sympathetic as William, it can make the story more interesting if the reader can feel sorry for them and understand why they did what they did. ("I *had* to train tigers to guard my mansion! I own lots of valuable stuff, and I needed to make sure no one tried to rob me!")

- *Make the culprit a real villain.* You might also do the opposite of making the culprit sympathetic. It can be a lot of fun to make them into a big villain when they confess. What the villain is saying might be so strange, or the speech they're giving is so evil, it's just plain fun to read—and to write. ("Once I have an army of trained tigers, I'll be able to go

264

shopping wherever I want and never have to pay for anything! Nobody will dare to stand in my way!")

- *Explain how the mystery happened in more detail.* Sometimes the detective catches the culprit, but the mystery is so weird they still don't understand exactly how it happened, and they need the culprit to explain. ("I suppose you're still wondering how I trained all those tigers in the first place? You see, I used to be the owner of a zoo, which was when I made a startling discovery about how to communicate with big cats. . . .")

Finally, every confession has **consequences.** In a lot of mysteries, the consequences are simple: The culprit goes to jail.

This has been done OVER AND OVER AGAIN, however, and there are many more interesting ways for a mystery to turn out. That doesn't mean every mystery needs to be as weird as "the culprit must take his plant that turns people into dogs back to his island, to avert chaos." But you should try to make the consequences more surprising than "jail." Maybe the culprit needs to do something to apologize for the mystery. ("I'll donate the treasure I found to get all the pools in town fixed again.") Maybe the culprit was doing something good all along, and everyone else needs to make it up to *them.* ("I drove my spaceship to Earth to help you. Now that you've found me, I need your help to make it back home.") Or now that the mystery has been solved, maybe there's an even bigger, more dangerous secret that's been uncovered, and must be dealt with. ("It turns out I trained the tigers too well. Soon, they'll be smarter than any human who ever lived, and I'm scared of what they're planning.")

IDEA STORM: GET A CONFESSION, AND DECIDE ON THE CONSEQUENCES

It's the moment you've been planning for since way back in the beginning: the **end**! Now you just need to explain to your readers how all the clues fit together, and tell them about your culprit.

Think about how you want your culprit to **confess.** Are they going to tell a story that makes them sympathetic to the reader? Or are they going to turn out to be a real villain? Maybe they'll clear up some final details about how the mystery happened?

What will the **consequences** be? Try to find some consequences that are different, and more interesting than "jail." One place to start is to look back at your Culprit Case File (see page 220) at the question: "What will happen if someone finds out this person is the culprit?" If you already had an interesting idea listed there, use it!

🔍 DETECTIVE'S NOTEBOOK:
JUST WHEN YOU THOUGHT IT WAS SAFE

Ahhhh, finally time to relax after a job well—uh-oh.

In some mysteries, just when you think the case has been solved, and everything is over, suddenly the detective is in danger once again. In Eliza's case, it's because Leif has realized how valuable the berries from that rare plant would be, and wants to keep some for himself . . . even if it means he has to push Eliza out the window so she can't tell anyone.

There are a lot of different places this sudden danger could come from at the end of a mystery. Here are a few examples:

- The culprit escapes, or the culprit confesses, but then immediately tries to get revenge on the detective.
- The culprit goes away . . . but they secretly had a helper in the setting that the detective didn't know about! This helper is very angry now.
- The case is solved, but there's a new danger in the setting. For example, we finally know that the tiger in the restaurant escaped from the mansion . . . but now the detective is stuck in the mansion, surrounded by super-intelligent angry tigers. Or we finally found out why all the water was missing

from the swimming pools, but now the culprit accidentally caused a flood, and the town is in danger!

 **IDEA STORM: WRITE ONE LAST SURPRISE**

Do you want to put your detective in sudden danger at the very end of the story? Think about what might put them in danger: Is it the culprit? A friend or helper of the culprit's who we didn't know about? Is it some other danger in the setting?

How does the detective get past this sudden danger? You can look back at "Detective's Notebook: Running Into an Unexpected Obstacle" on page 248 for more ideas about how to get the detective back to safety! As always: you have PERMISSION TO GET WEIRD!

DETECTIVE'S NOTEBOOK: A MYSTERIOUS PROLOGUE, REVISITED

Secrets love three things . . .

We're finally at the end! So what was happening in that mysterious prologue? Go back and read it one more time.

After reading the whole book, you'll probably have a much clearer idea than when you started.

Did you do it? Here were the basics: Leif and his crew arrived at the docks in their boat. They unloaded their plants into a truck and drove away. Then William snuck out of the boat, turned into a wolf, and chased after the truck (*"one secret following another"*).

It seems so obvious, now that you've read everything! But it took a whole lot of careful planning to get there.

 IDEA STORM: MYSTERIOUS PROLOGUE

How do you write your own mysterious prologue? This is your biggest mystery writer challenge of all:

1. Finish a whole mystery story! Seriously, your mysterious prologue will work much better if you know *exactly* what's going to happen in the story.
2. Think about what happens *before* your story begins. What interesting secrets are in the setting, which may eventually have something to do with the mystery? Is there suspicious behavior happening? Some mysterious prologues show us what it's like when the mystery first happens . . . even if they don't give too many clues about *how* it happened, or who caused it.

3. Tease the reader. Tell them just a *little* bit about the secrets you're hiding. Not too much (definitely not so much they can guess the culprit). Just enough to get them hooked.

This is the last Idea Storm. Did you do them all? If so . . .

CONGRATULATIONS!
YOU JUST WROTE A MYSTERY!

If you followed along the whole way, then you:

- Came up with a setting
- Imagined a mystery in that setting
- Created a detective to solve the mystery
- Decided on a culprit who caused the mystery—but kept the culprit's identity TOP SECRET
- Carefully chose which clues you wanted the detective to find
- Planned an investigation, in which the detective looked for clues by snooping around, watching out for suspicious behavior, identifying suspects, following leads, and questioning witnesses
- Added excitement to the investigation by having the culprit strike again and the detective run into an unexpected obstacle, and possibly by wrapping it up with a sting operation

- Cracked the case, got a confession, and had interesting consequences (just when your reader thought it was safe . . .)
- Finally, you brought it full circle, and wrote a mysterious prologue to **begin** the story.

What can you do now?

Go back to the beginning, and make it even better! Now that you've finished the end, you may find ways to make the whole story even more exciting! Make your writing more suspenseful, put in even more interesting clues, find the perfect piece of suspicious behavior to lead the detective toward the suspect. . . .

OR

Start an even WEIRDER story, with a more baffling mystery, a more unexpected suspect, and the most peculiar trail of clues that any detective has ever had to follow.

OR

Give yourself a high five for a job well done! But secretly . . . be thinking of more mysterious similes, and suspenseful paragraphs, and cryptic riddles. Keep sharpening that mystery-writer brain for the next time inspiration strikes!

MYSTERY CREATION ZONE

APPENDIX:
PHOEBE'S ORIGINAL IDEA (WITH SPOILERS!)

Here's the complete idea that Phoebe originally submitted for *Digging Up Danger*.

If you haven't read the whole story yet, ARE YOU SURE YOU WANT TO READ THIS? Because there are spoilers. Don't say we didn't warn you. It's not too late to turn back! Okay, here it is.

> Wait a minute! One thing on Phoebe's planning sheet is not exactly the same as what happened in Digging Up Danger. Do you notice where it's different?

When you're writing, sometimes the ideas that first sparked your story might change and grow while you work. That's what happened with *Digging Up Danger*: Jacqueline West started writing, using all of Phoebe's ideas for inspiration, but then she got this WEIRD idea about what the plant's mysterious powers could be (if you've read all the way through, you know what I mean!), and decided to chase after it and see where it took the story. Eventually, things got SO weird she decided this one detail about why the culprit caused the mystery didn't exactly fit the story anymore. That's totally okay—letting your imagination run wild might mean that you have to change around your original plans!

☠ THE SPARK: WHAT SHOULD THE MYSTERY BE ABOUT? ☠

THE MYSTERY (pick one or both!) There is something in your setting that is MISSING. What is it? There is something WEIRD in your setting that shouldn't be there. What is it?

In a plant store, in New York City, that held strange, exotic plants from all over the world, there was the rarest plant in the world. Not too many people knew about it because it was still being studied for its strange properties. It was stolen...

What made it rare was that it was from an island where not too many people lived and many were afraid to visit. You can only get to the island by boat.

SETTING

The setting is the plant store in NYC, the neighborhood surrounding the plant shop, and the island.

Who is your DETECTIVE?

There are two detectives: a scientist, who was coming to study the plant, and her daughter, who is a teenager and works at the plant shop.

What is one DETAIL about your detective that is funny and/or surprising?

When the daughter was nervous she would always take a break to stretch.

Who is the CULPRIT? This is who caused the mystery in the first place either by taking something or making something disappear from the setting, or putting something weird there that didn't belong.

The culprit is someone originally from the island who recognized the plant and knew that it was special.

WHY did the culprit do it?

He couldn't afford to support his family enough, and he knew he could use the plant and sell it for a lot of money.

What is one DETAIL about the culprit that is funny and/or surprising?

He always wears a hat and sunglasses because he doesn't like the sun. When he takes off his sunglasses, you see that his eyes are yellow. People from the island have yellow eyes.

CLASSIFIED
ANSWER KEY

MYSTERY WRITER CHALLENGE:

Setting the Scene

1. The beach
2. An amusement park. The screams were from a roller coaster!

MYSTERY WRITER CHALLENGE:

Making Up a Mystery

12 mysterious bananas

MYSTERY WRITER CHALLENGE:

The Right Clues for You

1. A clown

2. A dentist (the minty string was dental floss)

3. A super strong robot with wheels instead of legs (the note was written in "binary," a language used by computers with ones and zeros instead of letters of the alphabet)

MYSTERY WRITER CHALLENGE:

Where Will the Clues Lead?

1. A pizza restaurant

2. Somewhere with lots of dogs. A dog pound, dog kennel, dog park, or doggy day care. The detective will just have to see which of those might be nearby.

MYSTERY WRITER CHALLENGE:

Catching the Witness in a Lie

1. In the middle of the night with no power, no moon, no stars or flashlight to see by, how did this person see a clown through a window 100 feet away? Even if they somehow saw the clown, how in the world would they be able to see dark blue beanbags?

2. There was no Internet in 1979.

MYSTERY CREATION ZONE

GET STUCK BACK IN TIME WITH

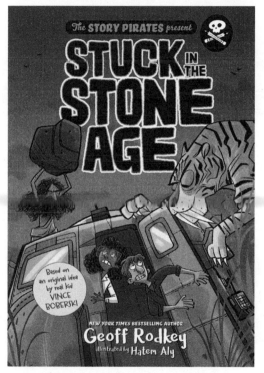

Read on for a peek at

STUCK IN THE STONE AGE

Show and Tells were the most exciting thing about working at CEASE. When a scientist's latest discovery was ready to share with others, they held a Show and Tell for everyone at the center. What began at a CEASE Show and Tell often ended in a Nobel Prize, a world-changing new product, a billion-dollar company, or all of the above.

When she walked into the director's office, Marisa was so excited she could hardly breathe.

"Dr. Palindrome?"

"Hello! Dr. . . . Murray, isn't it?"

"Morice, actually."

"Right! Michelle Morice!"

"Marisa Morice."

"Sorry! It takes me a little while to learn names."

"I've been here for ten years."

"And we're SO glad to have you! What can I help you with, Marina?"

Marisa didn't bother to correct him again. He'd remember her name soon enough. "I'd like to schedule a Show and Tell?"

"Wonderful! How soon?"

"As soon as possible?"

Dr. Palindrome checked his calendar. "How about tomorrow?"

"Okay. Great!"

"Super! Dr. Vasquez is also doing a Show and Tell. So we'll combine the two. A double feature!"

Marisa's heart leaped. Maybe tomorrow would be the day she and Dr. Vasquez finally had lunch! "Sure thing!"

Then she thought about it some more, and her excitement turned to worry. Marisa had no idea what Dr. Vasquez had planned. What if it upstaged Marisa's big invention?

No. How could that be? Marisa had worked on hers for ten years! It had to be at least as good as whatever Dr. Vasquez had planned. There was no reason to worry.

But Marisa worried anyway.

🐾🐾🐾

The next afternoon, fifty-eight scientists and a janitor

gathered in CEASE's auditorium for its first-ever double Show and Tell.

Marisa and Dr. Vasquez stood on the stage with Dr. Palindrome. Marisa stood next to a small table, covered in a black sheet. Dr. Vasquez, her fingernails painted the perfect shade of red for the occasion, stood next to a wheeled cart topped by a mysterious giant box the size of a double-wide refrigerator. It was covered in a much larger (and, Marisa had to admit, much nicer) black sheet than Marisa's.

"So!" Dr. Palindrome's voice boomed. "What will you two be showing us today?"

"You first," said Dr. Vasquez to Marisa with a friendly smile.

"Ummm . . . okay."

Marisa stepped forward, her whole body trembling. It was only her confidence in the invention she was announcing that kept her from either fainting or running from the room.

Her voice barely rose above a whisper. Even through the microphone, the other scientists had to strain to hear her.

"I've . . . um . . . built a working solar-cell prototype—" Marisa felt herself getting dizzy and had to pause for a moment to breathe—"that combines graphene and molybdenum disulfide to a thickness of twenty thousand nanometers."

Marisa pulled the black sheet off the table to reveal a solar panel the size and shape of a small windowpane.

A murmur of surprise went through the crowd. There was even a gasp or two.

"That's AMAZING!" yelled Tom. "What does it mean?"

"It's, um, ten times more efficient than current panels," Marisa answered. "So, um, it's, uh, kind of a revolution in solar energy. That, um, will solve mankind's energy needs forever with, um, zero harm to the environment."

"OHMYGOSH!" yelled Tom. "That is DEFINITELY AMAZING!" He looked around. "Right?"

Tom was right. The other scientists were all nodding, smiling, and whispering to each other with excitement.

As she watched them from the stage, Marisa's nervousness melted away. Her face could barely contain her smile.

Just look at them! They were so excited! They loved her invention! Even Dr. Vasquez was beaming, and she'd just been upstaged!

This was the moment Marisa had been waiting ten years to enjoy.

It felt even better than she'd dreamed. The scientists were all waving their hands in the air, desperate to quiz her about the solar panels. Or possibly to invite her to lunch! She wasn't sure which. But she couldn't wait to find out.

Dr. Palindrome cleared his throat, quieting the crowd. "Now, I'm sure you all have a lot of questions for Dr. Moran—"

"Morice," Marisa corrected him, with a confidence that surprised even her. "Sorry."

"Not at all! Morice! Right! My apologies. But before we get to the questions, let's not forget Dr. Vasquez. Have you got something for us that's even more amazing than a solution to all of mankind's energy needs?"

"I think I do," said Dr. Vasquez. "I've invented a time machine."

She whipped the sheet off her giant box, revealing a six-foot-tall, five-foot-wide contraption made of metal and glass.

The room exploded with noise as fifty-seven scientists and a janitor went completely bonkers.

"WHAAAAAAAT?"

"OHMYGOSH!"

ACKNOWLEDGMENTS

We would like to especially acknowledge our Education Director Quinton Johnson, whose brilliant pedagogies underlie the Mystery Creation Zone, and without whom the Story Pirates would not be teaching creative writing in such a dynamic, engaging, and effective way.

We would also like to thank the following friends, colleagues, and champions (in no particular order): Stephen Barbara, Rhea Lyons, Derek Evans, Charlie Russo, Sam Forman, Adrienne Becker, Laura Heywood, Allen Hubby, Eric Cipra, Jon Glickman, Natalie Tucker, Nicole Brodeur, The Drama Book Shop, Geoff Rodkey, Jason Wells, Joanna Campbell, Danielle Chiotti, Gimlet Media, Simon Shaw, Maggie Pisacane, Mark Merriman, Marcie Cleary, Mara Canner, Brandon York, Bekah Nutt, Jennifer and Geoff Wolinetz, Austin Sanders, Louie Pearlman, Meg McDermott, Will Cooper, Jess Boonstra, Amy Gargan, Bailey David Johnson, Lynn Weingarten, and the hundreds of thousands of kids who have sent us their stories since 2004.

DO YOU WANT MORE STORY PIRATES IN YOUR LIFE?

Check out our free podcast! You can hear additional stories written by kids just like you, performed by the hilarious Story Pirates and friends. PLUS: we interview real kid authors about their writing process!

Find out why the *New York Times* and *Today* call it one of the best podcasts for kids.

Download the Story Pirates Podcast today on any podcast app—or ask your parents to say "Story Pirates Podcast" into their smart speaker!

Check out the Story Pirates Podcast!